What REMAINS

—— In the Wilderness ——

B.R. GOODWIN

Copyright © 2021 B.R. Goodwin.

All rights reserved. No part of this book may be used or reproduced by any means, graphic, electronic, or mechanical, including photocopying, recording, taping or by any information storage retrieval system without the written permission of the author except in the case of brief quotations embodied in critical articles and reviews.

This is a work of fiction. All of the characters, names, incidents, organizations, and dialogue in this novel are either the products of the author's imagination or are used fictitiously.

WestBow Press books may be ordered through booksellers or by contacting:

WestBow Press
A Division of Thomas Nelson & Zondervan
1663 Liberty Drive
Bloomington, IN 47403
www.westbowpress.com
844-714-3454

Because of the dynamic nature of the Internet, any web addresses or links contained in this book may have changed since publication and may no longer be valid. The views expressed in this work are solely those of the author and do not necessarily reflect the views of the publisher, and the publisher hereby disclaims any responsibility for them.

Any people depicted in stock imagery provided by Getty Images are models, and such images are being used for illustrative purposes only. Certain stock imagery © Getty Images.

Interior Image Credit: Jessica Lewis

Scripture quotations are from the ESV® Bible (The Holy Bible, English Standard Version®), copyright © 2001 by Crossway, a publishing ministry of Good News Publishers. Used by permission. All rights reserved.

ISBN: 978-1-6642-2640-1 (sc)
ISBN: 978-1-6642-2642-5 (hc)
ISBN: 978-1-6642-2641-8 (e)

Library of Congress Control Number: 2021904618

Print information available on the last page.

WestBow Press rev. date: 04/27/2021

For my husband, Lawrence.
So much of you is scattered throughout these pages.
Thank you for being my constant encourager
and for pointing me to Christ in all things.

Special Thanks to Jessica Lewis,
who brought life to this story through her illustrations.

Chapter 1

Running. Would we ever stop running?

I can't remember the last time I felt settled. Like I had an actual home, without the threat of being forced out or found. Something permanent. Something lasting. Before my life changed completely, I never ran for fun, like so many of my friends did. In gym class, I'd make up an excuse to run behind the bleachers where the nearest garbage can waited for me, throwing up whatever I'd eaten for breakfast that morning. I loathed running and dreaded those gym days where I knew it'd be required of me. It seemed so effortless to my friends, and it was no secret to any of us how very, very bad I was at it.

Now though, it feels like all I ever do is run. And I've gotten surprisingly good at running. From a campsite in the woods to a dinky motel, through fields and forests, in the dark. I'm inherently unsettled. The worst part of it all, I think, is that I'm not sure what I'm running towards anymore. Survival. Freedom. Death. I find myself so often thinking or, more so wishing—what I wouldn't give to be in that gym class right now. Running for *fun* and not out of fear.

The day I left home and my life as a nomad began started like any Thursday morning. Breakfast, a minor argument with my mom about why taking my little brother to school was the bane of my existence, classes, lunch with friends. I remember laughing at Jamie Fratz, as she chased a freshman out of the lunchroom when he finished a dare to kiss her. Thankful to not be the center of that sort of attention, I joined in on the laughter and chatter after the fact —teasing a blushing, flustered Jamie as she came back to her seat, setting wedding dates and naming their future children. But then, as the laughter faded and we scarfed the rest of our lunches down before the end of lunch bell sounded—the names were called.

I knew exactly what was happening as soon as they were called over the ancient loud speaker of my four hundred-population high school. Everyone did. I had been warned for what felt like my whole life that this day would come. Silence fell over what had been a rambling, crowded lunchroom only seconds before.

"Brian Acworth…Luca Alexis….Janel Creel… Emma Dates"

I knew them. Knew them all. Brian and I grew up together in our tiny hometown, sharing Sunday school classes since preschool. He was a senior, popular and athletic, and friends with everyone he met. Luca was another senior, who had been sitting beside Brian. He was quiet and generally somber, or maybe shy. He was Brian's friend from camp who moved to our small town two years before. Janel was a pretty freshman. Emma, another senior, was smart, beautiful, and admired by most of the boys in our school.

Heart pounding and body frozen, all I could do was wait. Wait to hear my name. To hear my brother's name. I counted in my head as they were read off by my school counselor's voice.

Knowing there would be fourteen names she'd spill out in her monotone, bored tone.

"James Griffith...Samantha Hall (my best friend)...Lincoln Kale (her boyfriend)" And then Caleb. "Caleb Lee."

My baby brother's name stung as it rang for the whole school to hear. Recognizing that I'd be next, I unconsciously held my breath, every second knowing my seventeen-year-old life would never be the same.

And the familiar, droning voice spoke again, "Vala Lee."

The air pierced with it. Vala. Vala. Chosen. That's what my name meant. Growing up, my parents always said phrases like, "Vala, God chose you for something special," or, "You were chosen to be our daughter." They made sure I knew its significance. That I was chosen.

Vala Lee. Chosen.

I was chosen to or told to, immediately report to our school's gym with thirteen other seemingly unimportant names. Ironic, given my dislike for that particular place. But our names were not unimportant. When called out, all who listened knew what it meant. Knew what we were chosen for. I remember the deep exhale that came, as if I had been near the brink of suffocation with it. Heart pounding, fighting the tears that I knew I wanted to shed, and would eventually come, I listened to that voice; stale, filling the air of the cafeteria, finishing its mission.

The final five names rang out. Calling on two twin boys from my class, a sophomore girl, and two freshmen, a boy and a girl who immediately and quietly stood and began the short walk to our school's gym. I stood too, but only after watching the others and feeling the quiet, piercing glances from Jamie and those around me who were still safely in their seats. Knowing their eyes would watch us until we were gone, I walked purposefully to the cafeteria door, the last to leave. I shut the door behind me and began the walk down the eerily quiet hallway toward the gym.

It's funny the things that have stuck with me from that day. The strange details I seem to remember. I can't recall how I physically could carry myself down the hallway, but I do remember the chipping, beige-colored paint peeling from the edges of brick along the wall. The hall smelled of pungent cleaning supplies, as if a mess had recently been cleaned during the now distant lunch hour. I remember the feeling of uncertainty my feet walked with, unsteady and unfamiliar, dragging heavily beneath me.

I watched ahead of me as Sam and Lincoln walked silently hand in hand. Sam's dark hair swung from her pony tail with every step they took. Steps in unison with hers, Lincoln seemed to continuously glance toward Sam as he led her to their destination. Watching them made me wish I had someone walking along beside me, if only to help hold me up the rest of the way. I remember the look of the faces of the other thirteen students nervously glancing at me as I entered the gymnasium last, and alone.

Ms. Green, the school's secretary, waited for us in the gym. A mousy woman, her thin hair tousled across her eyebrow as she nervously paced her feet back and forth on the wood floor. Her clothes looked slightly disheveled, as they often did. And I noticed her gray cardigan looked as if it was buttoned at the top in an unmatched hole. She was always kind to the students as one of the administrators in the main office of the high school, but I knew her sympathies were likely buried deep to complete her assignment. She looked uncomfortable, standing a safe distance from the member of the Guard, who had been sent to gather us. He stood much taller than her, in a dark suit and looked foreboding there next to her.

He alone spoke to us, militant and disconnected, "Collect your bags and line up at the wall. Instructions will follow."

Ms. Green avoided our eyes and looked at the manila folders in her hands with what I'm sure had our names written on their tabs. She handed each folder to the guardsman as he called out our names again. She looked conflicted, but I knew she would say nothing. Her silence, like so many others, stands out in my memory of that day. It resonated long after we were released from the school.

After issuing each of us a numbered bag and instructions of the acceptable belongings that may be placed within them, we were told by the guard member to immediately go home. The numbers, I assumed, were their method to label and track us. We would be picked up from our individual homes within hours.

He radioed his superiors in front of us, "Stage one complete in section four."

Emma spoke up in the silence, only broken previously by the guardsman, "What's stage one? How many are there?" Emma's beauty did little to cloak her fear as she looked back and forth between the faces nearest her.

The suited man ignored Emma completely, "You are permitted three minutes to say goodbye." It was an act of mercy we had not expected.

I knew I would not be entering into that gym again, at least not as a student. Grabbing the pale-green and brown bag, marked seven, I couldn't help but wonder how many of us there really were. Our numbers were all out of order and the highest went to twenty-five, which one of the Warden twins had strapped to his back as he nervously paced beside his brother. How many numbered bookbags were being forced upon other teenagers at this exact moment? And, as Emma had vocalized what I'm sure we all were thinking...*What would come next?*

Getting to Caleb as quickly as allowed, I dragged him by the bag labeled with a twenty-one attached to his back, to the spot in the gym where Sam and Lincoln stood, saying their goodbyes. Their silent, scared faces painted a portrait of dread. Lincoln, who was always so put together, looked uncharacteristically frazzled and his dark brown skin seemed grey and sickly with stress.

In middle school, Linc was a finalist in our school's spelling bee. We were invited to watch the last three contestants in the auditorium from an audience of bleachers as they stood on stage regurgitating the spelling of words like "catastrophe" and "omnipotent." I had been nervous just watching him fumble about on the stage, twisting his hands together each time his turn came. He won, which came as no surprise to anyone who knew him, but it had been painful to watch him act so uncomfortably.

He looked similar to how he had on that stage. His face drained of its color and his body showing signs of nervous twitching, even in the midst of comforting Sam. His thin arms wrapped around her, towering over her much smaller frame. He whispered quickly into her ear. Sam's head, although nuzzled into Linc's chest, nodded in agreement with whatever words he spoke to her.

When they separated, Sam's dark hair was tousled, loosening her pony tail in an effortlessly beautiful way. She put her hand out to me and drew Caleb and I into their small circle. Not knowing exactly what lay ahead, I hugged them both, unsure of when I would see my friends again.

Sam whispered in my ear, "It's okay Vala. I'll see you soon." Sam's cup was always half full, a trait I admired in her. I knew it was wishful thinking, but I hoped what she said was true.

I noticed Linc move towards Luca, who had been awkwardly watching our goodbyes nearby. They spoke quietly near us for a minute. Luca had only been in our town for two years, but he and Linc had grown close quickly. He was taller than Linc and always quiet. He held his assigned number one bag in his hand, letting it hang at his side as he talked somberly with Linc. Where Linc seemed stressed and out of character, Luca was seemingly calm and collected. We hadn't interacted much in the past two years, but I noticed him look concerningly towards Sam, Caleb, and I as he and Linc spoke, and then hugged Linc quickly before turning to leave.

One of the guardsmen abruptly yelled, "Time's up!" And the low chatter that had momentarily filled the gym silenced completely. With my stomach in knots, it was hard to release Sam's hand as she held mine.

Caleb though, gentle and strong, pulled me away whispering quietly, "Come on, Vala. It's time." He ushered me towards the gym's exit, walking us into a back parking lot. The cement had cracked with weeds pushing through and the yellow lines were faded from years of wear. For the first time since we were toddlers, walking through the grocery store with our mother or down the street to a neighbor's house, I held Caleb's hand as we left the school grounds. Holding each other steady for the arduous walk home.

We walked as quickly as possible. Silently. Listening to the normal, everyday sounds along the highway that led to the home we both had lived in our entire lives. Afraid to catch the glances from passersby at the packs on our backs, I embarrassedly looked straight ahead. The world around us would continue to turn despite the turmoil I knew was waiting after our walk home.

As we walked up the dirt path leading to the house, I stole a peek at Caleb, just in time to see the streaks tears had made down the sides of his cheeks. I admired the way he didn't wipe away the stream of tears from his face. My brother was not one to be embarrassed or nervous. I felt his quiet bravery in that moment, him leading me, up the steps and through the front door of our small home. That morning's argument about driving Caleb to school was long forgotten and seemed so trivial. I knew whatever lay ahead I couldn't be alone. I felt safe with someone by my side.

With Caleb by my side.

Chapter 2

A QUIET CHAOS MET US AS WE WALKED THROUGH THE FRONT door. The kind of quiet that tantalizes your nerves, birthing a deep pit in your gut that makes you want to hide until it passes. But I knew, even then, that this chaos would not pass. It was only beginning.

Those who had talked about this day, anticipating its possibility, had prepared. Food. Water. Packed bags and a plan with an escape strategy. My parents were as prepared as they could be. They decisively scattered around the house like worker ants gathering our last minute supplies. My mom, pregnant with what I referred to as her mid-life baby, looked almost lyrical as she grabbed a blanket, flashlight, and batteries, and in one swoop shoved them into a small red bag. One that had been overused for years of countless camping trips. Her thick, dirty-blonde hair sat on top of her head in a half pulled-out bun. She brushed some stray hairs from across her forehead and hardly noticed us as

Caleb and I walked into the house, only realizing we were there when her fluttering was interrupted by the sound of Dad's voice,

"Vala, When did it happen?" He asked.

I shook myself from the trance I had been in at what I thought was such a strange question. He had broken the silence after our deafeningly, quiet walk and entrance into the house.

Mama abandoned her work and scurried over to hug us both, as I answered Dad, "It started at lunchtime. Maybe around eleven thirty, I guess. We were in the cafeteria and then they sent us to the gym."

I looked to Caleb with uncertainty, who nodded in agreement and added, "They'll be here soon."

Mama took a minute to rub her hand down my cheek, her other hand holding Caleb's beside me, "Sweet girl, everything's going to be alright. Okay?" She smiled, gave Caleb's hand a knowing squeeze, and went back to her work.

After exchanging hugs and a few quick instructions with Dad, I watched as he set our kitchen timer for one hour and we all set out to do the tasks that we had been prepared for so many years ago. We worked swiftly, but silently, each with our own assignment to carry out. The quiet in the house drowned in the ticking of that kitchen timer.

Tick. Tick. Tick. Tick.

For what seemed like forever I listened. Listened to the clock ticking over the thousands of thoughts running through my brain. Listened to the hurried footsteps of my family as they went about their duties. Frozen in my little solitary moment, but not really frozen as I could hear that clock ticking away the last moments I would spend in the house my parents had brought me home to as a baby. Where I had taken my first steps. Where I watched my mama's feet dance around her pale yellow kitchen as she expertly cooked our meals. Where I laughed with Caleb as we chased each other in and out of rooms as kids. And where we spent hot summer nights catching fireflies in mason jars with Daddy as Mama watched from our back porch swing.

I breathed it in. I wished I could stay in my little moment, but was reminded by the *tick tick tick* of that mint green clock hanging from our refrigerator, that the alarm would sound in less than an hour. And I had things to do.

One of my jobs was to retrieve our packed bags from a safe spot we had hidden them in, just months before. We would need the supplies inside to live off of, wherever we were going. Our parents had a plan, but hadn't shared much with us. Only that, the less we knew, the better.

When the raids started years ago, they were few and far between. The first raid happened on a Tuesday night in November. I was finishing up homework at the kitchen table. Mom and Dad cleaned the mess dinner had made while simultaneously arguing with Caleb over a book report he hadn't turned in. They hardly heard the knock at the door, but I did. Something about it was unfamiliar, forceful, too consistent. Jumping to answer it before someone else could, I was greeted by two men dressed in plain business suits, asking to speak to an adult. Annoyed that my curiosity about their visit may not be answered directly, I called Dad to the door, only to be shoved behind him as he stepped out onto the porch closing the door as he left.

My dad had always been a calm man, generally. Thinking long before he said anything. He defended his side of an argument sternly and tactfully, rarely raising his voice. But on this night, it was not more than three minutes before I heard the strange, unfamiliar sound of his voice rising, in anger and in what I now know was fear. Dad was forced to stay outside as the men came into the house, directing us aggressively to step outside while they performed a routine search.

For twenty minutes we waited in the November chill as strangers rummaged through our belongings. Searching for any paraphernalia they deemed illegal and anything that linked us to the group referred to as *the Remnant*. When they were finally gone our house was left in shambles. Pictures were strewn across the floor, everything was taken off of shelves and from drawers, and everything on or in cabinets was scraped from their places. A giant red *R* was spray painted on our door, left to inform the neighbors surrounding us of our rebellion and who we belonged to.

We were not prepared that night, but were let off with a warning as they left our house pummeled, carrying a trash bag full of our unsanctioned personals that *posed a threat to peace and equality*: jewelry, photographs, wall hangings, art, and treasured books. I remember how Mama had mourned the loss of her most precious Bible, given to her by her grandmother. The deep blue leather of the exterior had long worn away around its edges, and the contents of its thin pages were highlighted and noted upon by both women. It had stayed open, more often than not, on her bedside table, but had been thrown carelessly into the depths of their trash bags in the raid. It was one of the many tokens of our life regarded as a threat by the government.

We found out at school the next day that other families, like ours, were not so lucky. Brian's dad was beat in front of his family that same night, attempting to stand up to the men that entered their home. I remember the pit that grew inside of my stomach as he told us of how he held his mom and two younger sisters in his arms as they screamed, begging the men to stop. His dad had recovered, but the trauma of the attack remained. Brian was terrified and angry. Rightfully so. And I was too. What would happen to us if we were caught again?

After the first raid we became much more careful about the items we knew would not be acceptable to the men we later learned were members of the Guard. Hiding those possessions behind light sockets and under floorboards. We started to meet for prayer and study in secret places, basements, back rooms of sympathetic coffee shops or restaurants. And, after *R*'s were subsequently engraved on driveways, on front door frames, and mailboxes, we knew the trust of our neighbors couldn't be expected if our worst fears became reality. Many members lost their jobs, with employers nervous to maintain even working relationships with anyone rebelling against the government. And others took their kids out of schools as even children sensed the change in the atmosphere. We couldn't run without those around us seeing. The Guard, I'm sure, felt confident that students would go directly home after stage one at the high school, because for many, there was nowhere else to go. In our small community, everyone knew if you were a member of the *Remnant*.

Some members had begun to deny their beliefs all together, but my family had not. We weren't ashamed of our convictions, but we sought to self-preserve. To keep our family safe. I sometimes wondered how we would tell people truth from the shadows, but fear stopped me from asking aloud. In the last year, the raids came more often, leading us to start our preparations and pack our safety bags in a storage container buried in the woods behind the house. I didn't know where we were to go, if anything happened, but I trusted that Dad and Mama did.

I grabbed a shovel from the spot I knew it would be in, leaning against the back of the house under the porch, and I started the short walk through an overgrown field to the woods. I set a quick pace with the shovel low to the ground and hoped against hope I would not raise attention from neighbors that may have been home from work already. Neighbors that would turn us in if they knew.

Chapter 3

I REACHED THE SECRET SPOT QUICKLY, REMEMBERING MY WAY using familiar trees as a road map. We'd spent summer days swinging by a rope across the ravine, cooling off in the water on hot days, and even camping under the shelter of the thousands of pines that stood through those woods. I was comfortable there. Dad brought me to this spot in the middle of the night at least two times before. Once to bury the bags and once to dig them up again to time me. It had been at least twenty minutes since the timer had been started and I knew the hole would take me roughly twelve to fifteen minutes to dig.

As I set to work, I prayed silently, knowing I would not have much time to finish my task. Surely, the Guard would be at the house to collect us soon. It was a warm April afternoon. Even under the shade of the woods, sweat dripped into my eyes as I hurriedly dug into the ground. When I finally felt the scrape of my shovel hit the storage container I paused to listen to another sound, one coming closer and closer to my spot in the trees.

The sound of men's footsteps, loud and unapologetic, just like the knock on our door so many years ago, became clearer and brisker. My stomach lurched into my throat. Throwing my pack on as quickly as possible, I threw myself behind a large oak, engulfed in kudzu. I watched as my father walked towards my tree with two men pushing at his sides. I held my breath as they came nearer, beseeching them silently not to come near the oak protecting our family's secret stash and the hole I had just dug behind me.

The men and the rifles they dug into his sides forced Daddy, strong and stoic, to the ground on his knees, facing my direction. His dark hair and clothes were tousled and the side of his face bore the marks of a beating. Could he see me? Could they see me? The two men, both dark, clean-shaven, and wearing the suits I knew meant they were members of the Guard, were too distracted badgering Dad with what I thought were questions to notice my spot behind the oak, or the sound of my heart beating louder than anything else that I could hear.

I'm not sure how long we were there in the woods, me hidden in the safety of the tree and its vines, and my father surrounded by these hunters of men. He said nothing from his knees and for a moment I thought he glanced at me. In the next though, Dad turned his face and spoke gently to one of the guardsmen, a tall and handsome young man, and was swiftly cut down by the force of only one bullet from the man's weapon. I could do nothing.

A scream caught in my throat and I covered my mouth with filthy, dirt-covered hands. I watched as the older man, stern and worn looking like old leather, kicked at my father's body to make sure it was lifeless. He callously turned to leave it there in the shadow of the oak trees. The young guardsman followed, reluctantly at first, as if hesitant to leave the traces of his crime to be found. Or maybe a sliver of his conscious felt the weight of his actions, but only for a moment. They abandoned his body on the floor of those woods, staring up into the blanket of spring leaves, barely blooming. I waited in shock to run to Daddy's body, until I could no longer hear their footsteps cracking twigs and leaves beneath them. I felt sure that even if I didn't move, they'd hear my heart pounding through my chest. When I could no longer hear or sense them near, I ran to him, falling on the ground at his side.

Time moved in slow motion as I sat beside my father, dressed in a green t-shirt and jeans, his eyes awake, but the rest of his body lay asleep — at peace. I'm not sure how long I sat before panic set in and reality punched me in the chest, so much so that I couldn't breathe. I shook uncontrollably. I felt cold with shock. And realized I didn't know how much time had passed since I had abandoned my post and my job, completely. It was late afternoon now, almost time for the sun to go down, and I couldn't bear to leave him alone in those woods, but I had to find Mama and Caleb. They should have met me by now in the woods, but no one had come. Waiting for darkness to come, I found my way back to our house as quickly and quietly as I could manage, tears still breaking through my vision as I fumbled my way through a basement window that we always left unlocked. A safeguard in our escape plan.

A safeguard. It all felt so pathetic now.

I think I knew. As soon as I climbed in through the window. I knew it was too quiet in the house. Too still. I allowed myself to hope though, knowing I had to see for myself. I could feel every creak of the wood beneath me as I climbed the basement stairs to whatever awaited me on the main floor of the house. It only took a moment to see the struggle that had taken place here. The bookbag Mama had been packing was strewn across the kitchen floor, along with pictures from our walls, and her precious china broken into tiny pieces.

Mama was so proud of that china set. It had been handed down to her from her grandmother and would eventually pass to me. It was elegant and simple, like her, and had a small print of a butterfly on the ridge of every dish. Mama always said that butterflies reminded her of new life, of something lovely being born from something painful. The only piece untouched was a little sugar server and the bronze spoon that paired with it, a butterfly floating near the top of the handle. Without really understanding why, I stored the spoon in my pocket, as I continued quietly through the kitchen into the living room.

And there, I found her.

My beautifully simple mother, lying as if asleep on the hardwood floor, with one hand cradling her waist and the baby brother or sister I would never meet. The leftover light from the sun fading away shown down on her through curtained windows. She looked like a painting, with her other hand draped carefully near her face. Like someone had posed her there purposefully to complete their masterpiece. She was lovely and she was gone. I forgot myself. Forgot the need for silence. For stealth. For escape.

And I let myself fall apart there on the hardwood floor, beside my mother in the yellow dress I had seen her floating around our kitchen in, only hours before. Weeping. Mourning. Forgetting to breathe. I protected her body with my own, unwilling to leave my place in the painting. Knowing this would be my last moments beside her, I kissed Mama's cheek and moved the wavy locks of dirty-blond hair from her face, as she had done to me so many times as a little girl, lovingly and tenderly admiring the beauty only a daughter can appreciate in her mother.

Overcome, I ran away from her spot on the floor to the hallway near our rooms, throwing up on the pale carpet we had always been taught to keep clean. I knew blood from her wounds had transferred to my hands and I manically scrubbed them against my jeans and the floor. And then, instinctively wiped my lips and the tears from my face.

I could hear voices in the distance.

First voices, then banging on doors. A child crying. Dishes breaking. Knowing the Guard must be looking for those who had escaped in neighboring houses, I ran quickly and quietly through the bedrooms of our home, searching for the only family I had left. Searching for Caleb.

He was gone. Along with his number twenty-one sack, I knew Caleb had been taken. And I thanked God for a moment that I wouldn't have to mourn him too. At least not now. Passing back through the house, I wouldn't let myself look over to Mama again. I couldn't. I left my own backpack, with the number seven patch sewed on its front pocket, behind. I was happy to rid myself of the labeled bag the Guard had provided. I grabbed the worn, red bookbag Mama had started packing instead, and shoved its contents back inside. The last thing I saw, before heading to the basement again for my escape window, was the mint-green timer still hanging on the refrigerator. The only thing, it seemed, untouched by that day.

Chapter 4

Finding Mama was the last time I let myself cry for a while. I stayed in the woods those first nights, beneath the oak tree that had protected me before. And I waited. Not eating. Not sleeping. Just waiting to be found, or to die maybe. I remained, paralyzed with fear and shock. I sat there in the middle of the kudzu-draped floor, of the woods I grew up playing in, knowing that my father's body was abandoned mere feet from me. And I could do nothing.

I was completely alone. I had no plan and I felt myself wishing I had been killed too. What would I do now? We had prepared, yes, but we hadn't talked about separation. About death. I grew up knowing my parents weren't afraid of death. They welcomed it. Even if it meant dying for what they believed in. We were taught not to fear, but something in me was always uneasy of their faith. Of the faith that they taught to Caleb. Of the faith they expected in me.

I always felt weaker than my little brother. Caleb was the light and Vala, the shadow. And I liked it that way. More than ever, I needed his light in those woods. He would have known what to do and I felt certain that he wouldn't have been paralyzed by the absolute fear and cowardice that I felt now.

When hunger and exhaustion finally overtook me, I decided to abandon my post beneath the oak tree and search the hole I dug, now days before, for supplies. It didn't take long to finish the hole, even as I took my time. Rummaging through my family's carefully prepared bags, I grabbed the essentials: a sweatshirt of mine that had been packed, another flashlight, a water bottle, the MREs my father had been given by a friend in the military, a little cash, one of Dad's flannel shirts, and a note in Mama's bag labeled, *for Vala and Caleb.*

Shaking from the hunger and the shock of this mysterious note, I fumbled to open it as quickly as possible.

> *Vala and Caleb,*
>
> *If you're reading this, we're probably gone. Know that we always thought this outcome was a possibility, but hoped we would remain with you both if we could. Take care of each other & don't fear the unknown, but take strength in knowing you both are a part of something larger than yourselves. We have faith that something beautiful can come from all of this and we pray that you will remember that truth in the days to come.*
>
> *Find the man named Micah, in Appalachia, where the creek bed glows at the mouth. Trust him. And hold on to the Hope that we have.*
>
> *We love you.*
>
> *Dad and Mom*

I reread it over and over until I had it memorized, struck with grief, and then with anger. They knew and never told us! They knew all along that we might end up alone. That I may end up alone. And they never said a word. Reading the letter reminded me of how alone I was and of how lost I was. My mind raised with questions. *Who was Micah? And where in the world was the creek bed that glows at the mouth. What did that even mean?*

Sitting in that hole and rereading my mother's handwriting, as I inhaled dried black beans and rice from an MRE, I didn't notice the footsteps behind me until it was almost too late. Running steps reached my tree just as I threw myself as far into the hole as possible, trying to hold my breath as they approached.

I knew it was more than one person, at the sound of their breaths gasping for air, but hidden from my view. Three people? Maybe four? I couldn't know and I wasn't brave enough to leave my hiding spot, until I heard a strange familiarity in the sounds of their whispers.

"Linc?"

Had I said that out loud? Silently cursing myself for being so stupid I allowed my eyes to peek over the hole's ledge, meeting the stares of Lincoln, Sam, Sam's younger sister Kate, and Luca Alexis. I knew I had caught Linc mid-sentence, but didn't care what I interrupted. Scrambling out of the spot with dirt crumbling in around me as I climbed, I almost tackled Sam with the weight and force of my body, hugging her and letting out a huge rush of air. I didn't realize I had been holding my breath, until I frantically breathed in the scent of her hair, letting myself feel relief for the first time in days.

Kate quickly joined us in the hug. At only ten years old, I had watched Kate grow up. She had always been a tomboy, Sam's opposite, but they had that *sister thing*, that I always wished for. They understood each other, in ways that even I, Sam's closest friend, could never really know. Kate's auburn hair was tied in a loose pony and a long sleeve shirt tied loosely around her waist.

She looked so much older now and I hoped her innocence had not been stripped as mine had, only days before. She made me long for Caleb more than I wanted to acknowledge. It hurt too much to think of him right now and where he might be.

Lincoln interrupted our silent hugging, with hurried whispers and more questions than I wanted to answer.

"How long have you been out here, Vala?

Are you hurt?

Have you eaten?

What was your escape plan?"

He whispered, but his tone was frantic, hurried and afraid. Lincoln had always been a detail guy. I knew he would make a plan for us and I trusted him, but I also did not want to dive into what I had endured over the past forty-eight hours. Avoiding each of his questions, I remembered they had been running.

"Were you being chased?" I asked with the same tone as Linc, but directed at the group.

"We were trying to reach a safe spot to sleep before nighttime," answered Kate, obviously surprising herself by speaking up before the others.

Confused, I began spurting off my own questions, "A safe spot? But, where are your parents? How long have you been running?"

A stampede of answers came from Lincoln, Sam, and Kate, all finishing each other sentences and explaining how their parents weren't even home when they arrived after school. Abandoned or orphaned, they weren't sure, and didn't stick around to find out. Sam and Kate met Lincoln within two hours of finding their empty house, at an arranged spot they set up in case of an emergency. Luca was already with him.

Luca, as quiet and brooding as ever, didn't chime in with his experience. He always played the observer in any of the times I had been around him. I barely knew him really. He offered up insight or answered questions willingly enough in class, and he was always respectful. Luca was smart and calculated, but he didn't seem to enjoy being around a lot of people.

Actually, a couple years before, I had a party at my house with friends from school while Mom and Dad had gone away for the weekend. Luca was still new to town then and I remembered how miserable he had been at my house that night. He looked like a foreigner in a strange land, meandering through our house while everyone else laughed, danced together, and played games. Ever since, he'd always kept his distance from others and a backseat role in anything at school.

In the woods that day though, he seemed in complete control. Just as he had been in the gym days before. Pacing back and forth behind the other three as they told their story, he searched the woods with his dark eyes and a stern look on his face. His blue shirt was torn, with what looked like blood stains covering the front of it. His brown hair, which he usually wore short with gel, lay disheveled atop his head. He looked fierce, compared to the other three's frightened faces. Like a lion protecting his den.

"Guys, we need to go now," Luca interrupted, just as Sam was explaining how they had come looking for my family, which brought them to the woods.

Almost thankful for the interruption, I turned towards Luca's spot in my woods. I knew if they had gone to my home looking for us, they had most likely seen Mama, and I couldn't bear to regurgitate those moments right now. Silence in the woods fell again, just as when I was alone, and we waited for Luca's direction.

"I'm glad you're okay, Vala," He acknowledged me briefly before continuing, "But we need to get somewhere safe for the night. I don't think we should risk waiting around here." He stammered a bit, as if embarrassed by his interruptions. It was maybe the most I had ever heard him speak.

I reassured them, although hesitantly, "No one has been here in a couple of days."

It was only then that they all seemed to notice the hole I had been in, and the opened bags and container scattered within.

"Are these your supplies? Can we go through them?" Lincoln asked, just as I saw Luca glance at my blood stained jeans and then in the direction of Daddy's body. The area I had been avoiding for days.

"Of course, um—yeah, you can take whatever you need," I answered choppily while I distractedly watched Luca inch his way closer to that spot in the woods.

I wish he hadn't seen it. Him. But none of the others seemed to notice.

As Lincoln, Sam, and Kate rummaged through my family's carefully packed belongings, I tried to meet Luca before he could reach Daddy's spot.

Meeting him there at the same time, Luca looked at me heartbroken.

"Do you know him? Is that your?" He hesitated with realization, "Vala…I…I'm sorry," Luca looked uncharacteristically crushed. Strong, but broken.

Hoping to sound as strong as he did, I avoided his eyes and barely got out the words, "…My dad." We stood beside each other silently. Still and daring not to look at each other after my admission.

He broke the silence saying, "That's not your blood on the front of your jeans is it?" He sounded worried and somber. I shook my head, still not daring to look at him. And then I felt Luca, the quiet guy I barely knew, put his hand over mine.

In that moment, I knew he understood somehow. Probably more than he wanted to.

Chapter 5

AFTER RANSACKING THE HOLE'S CONTENTS AND ASSURING them again that no one had been there, we collectively decided it would be safe to stay in my sanctuary for one more night. Lincoln and Luca separated quietly from us for a few minutes, obviously discussing something seriously as Sam, Kate, and I opened up an MRE for us all to share for dinner. As we prepared our tiny feast with *spicy penne pasta* printed on the label, Luca jumped into my hole and began to lift everything out to Lincoln, waiting above him. They worked, fighting against the spring sun setting, and a chill in the air greeting us with the night. After they finished dividing supplies into bags, and the sun was nearly gone, Lincoln and Luca laid Daddy to rest there, using one of their own blankets to carefully carry his body over the kudzu-covered ground.

No one spoke as they worked. I was grateful. Sam merely put her arm around my waist, pulling me close to her. I felt her body slightly trembling beside mine and I knew she was crying.

Touched by their gesture and as awkward as ever, I watched them, not really knowing how to respond. I can look back and know now that I was in complete shock. Orphaned and terrified, my body and mind couldn't comprehend the losses I suffered. But in my heart, I knew that both of my parents were at peace.

I was comforted in knowing Daddy was in the place that kept me safe these past days, but felt guilty wishing I could lie Mama beside him. What would become of her in our house? Who would find her there? As they finished their work, Lincoln grabbed Sam and Luca by the hand, and nodded towards Kate and I to do the same to finish the circle, as he led us in prayer. It was the first time since coming to the woods that I hadn't felt entirely alone.

That spring night was colder than the previous ones and I was ever thankful to have four warm bodies beside me. After eating our small meal and sitting quietly, whispering plans to each other and sharing with them my parent's letter, we soon felt the heaviness of the day. We slept next to the grave, with Lincoln and Luca taking turns as watchmen on each end. I woke in the early hours of the morning, while it was still dark, shivering and haunted by my days there. Not wanting to wake up Kate, who cradled herself between Sam and I all night, I laid still, staring at the early morning sky. Stars disappeared as a rosy, purple glow began to take their place. Kate's curled up body provided a bit of extra warmth in the early morning air that I welcomed. Feeling the weight of my eyes and previous days' events, I turned my head over for more sleep, meeting Luca's eyes staring at me. He shot a half smile at me as if he had been waiting there for a while.

Luca mouthed, "hi," to me and I self-consciously mouthed a silent, "hey," back. I noticed him shivering and immediately felt shame. I had not only a sweatshirt to fight the cool air, but had also drawn close to Daddy's flannel each night I had spent in the woods, all the while Luca had spent his nights in a tattered short-sleeve shirt. Reluctantly, I pushed the flannel near to his chest, holding my breath as I let the last bit of Daddy go to this almost stranger. He looked hesitant at first, to accept, but gave in to the cold. He sat up for only a moment to put it over his broad shoulders. Lying back down beside me, we stayed quiet for a long time. Neither willing to give in to sleep.

After some time, Luca broke the silence with a whisper, so as not to wake the peaceful sleepers beside us, "I'm so sorry, Vala. I know you've lost so much." Finally getting out the heartfelt apology that he didn't have to offer to me, but had tried so hard to give the day before, he seemed to relax. I did too.

And hoping he knew how sincerely I meant it, I responded, "I'm sorry too, Luca." I hadn't known what he had gone through, but he was clearly worn. And hurt. Whatever had happened.

It was the first time I think I ever said his name out loud. I'm sure I had said it in passing to Lincoln at some point, but never to Luca. His name was strong as it passed through my lips and I felt an odd security knowing he was a part of our group. I drifted slowly back to sleep, suddenly ultra-aware of the sound of my breathing next to Luca's steady breath and warmth beside me.

I dreamt of our home, there at the brink of the woods. Of a summer night, chasing a little boy around our backyard, with Caleb at my heels and Mama and Daddy laughing somewhere in the distance. The flicker of lightening bugs lit up the little boy's face as he giggled, with the carefree laugh only a child can have, untouched by the world. In an instant, though, the boy was gone, and I was left alone in those woods, searching frantically for the familiarity of the moments before.

"Find Micah, Vala," I heard Mama's voice somewhere in the darkness, "Find Caleb." Her voice taunted me as I searched, blindly, between the trees, hands outstretched and lost. And then I was falling. Back in the hole. Back in the grave, covered with dirt.

As I beat on the ground above me, screaming and covered in dirt, a voice beside me, Daddy's voice, whispered in my ear, "You have to find them, Vala. Find Them!"

I woke to Sam's gentle hand shaking me out of my nightmare. Cold, sweat-covered, and afraid, I hugged her instinctively, needing to assure myself of reality. I could still smell the dirt covering my face as it did in the dream, and realized my own filth for the first time in days. Closing my eyes, to avoid the embarrassment of the stares of the others, I asked her what time it was.

"Just after seven," she replied quietly.

She knew me so well. Well enough to know I wouldn't want to talk about my dream and that I'd want the attention off of me as soon as possible. She jumped up after holding me for long enough, wiped the hair from my face as a mother would and said, "Ok, we need to get going. Vala, pack up whatever you're bringing."

Her words brought the rest of the group out of the trance my screaming had placed them all in. I realized then, that they had all paused to look at me. I felt the heat of embarrassment rise in my cheeks and they all began to look busy again.

"Where are we going, Sam?" I asked, feeling like a small child looking for instruction. I glanced around and noticed that all of the bags were neatly piled beside the tree we slept under the night before, and a freshly-picked, small bouquet of spring wildflowers rested on Daddy's grave. I wondered who had taken the time to do such a thing in the midst of our impossible situation.

"*We* are heading to Appalachia, to find Micah, like the letter said," Lincoln answered.

"Of course you're going with us, Vala," chimed in Kate, grabbing onto my hand.

"I…I…I can't," I said quietly as the panic crept in, "Not yet, anyway. I have to find Caleb." Everyone fell silent and still, aside from Luca who seemed to hesitate, but then went on digging for something inside of his pack.

"Vala," Sam came near to me again, as a mother would to her child. She spoke with patience, soft-toned and gentle, "We went to your house yesterday, before we came to the woods."

She could barely look me in the eye, but I knew Kate and Lincoln were watching intently. I was thankful they hadn't mentioned my family before, but knew there was a reason they had never asked about my mom. I felt Kate's little hand squeeze mine.

"We don't even know if Caleb's alive," Lincoln joined us.

"We saw..." She began her argument as my head and heart screamed for her not to talk about her. To leave it alone. Buried. But Sam said the words I wished she wouldn't, "We saw your mama, Vala. And then with your dad...it just doesn't...," she trailed, avoiding my stare at this point.

"It doesn't seem likely that he's out there," Lincoln finished for her.

Luca avoided the conversation completely and I noticed Kate staring up at me, a tear streaming down her face. In that moment I hated the way she, Sam, and Linc all looked at me, with such pity. I preferred Luca's avoidance to their consolation. I was scared that I'd break at any second. Sam, too, caught my gaze and grabbed my other hand in hers, with a look of sadness that made me feel like an abandoned puppy in a wet cardboard box. She felt sorry for me. They all did.

"No!" I said, louder than I meant to and pulled instinctively away from them, "No, I am *going* to find Caleb. I have to." I was met with a cascade of arguments from Lincoln and Sam, as Kate watched us all, a worried look on her face. Luca continued to fidget in his bag and I began to feel defeated.

I didn't understand how they could even think to just abandon Caleb. One of us. My Brother. "You would look for Kate, Sam. You would never leave her behind—not knowing. I have to know what happened to him. I can't go without him." Searching for any argument I retorted, "Don't you want to know what happened to your parents?"

No one responded, but I noticed they looked more uncomfortable. Pleading with them now, I tried to make eye contact with Sam or Linc, "Please, Sammy," I grabbed her hand again, knowing I had crossed a line, "he's all I have left."

She tried to comfort me and I thought only of myself. I felt guilty before the words left my lips, and knew immediately by their reactions, that they were terrified to know the fate of their own parents.

Luca, finally abandoning the mysterious task inside his bag, stood up and directly looked at me—through me—and said, "Alright, Vala. I'll help you find Caleb," he gave Linc an understanding look and centered his attention on me, "and when you know—either way, we are going to Appalachia to find Micah. All of us are."

Chapter 6

On our first full day together we followed along the local highway through the woods, in the hopes of making our way back to the Hall's neighborhood. We'd need supplies to make it to wherever it was that we were going in our search for Caleb. I couldn't believe Linc and Sam agreed to help me, with just Luca on my side, but I was grateful. I knew I couldn't find him alone.

After much discussion, Lincoln and Luca thought we could find a way into the Hall's house easier than any of the others and look for any supplies that may be left. We camped in the woods, out of sight. Making camp along their street for a few days allowed us time to make sure there was no sign of the Guard patrolling the area. We took turns keeping watch at night, and slept in a row as we had near Daddy's grave on our first night together.

The guys took charge, making sure we had everything we needed, dividing our food, and trying their best to make us feel safe. The woods were becoming more familiar and I generally felt safe within them, hidden from the prying eyes of those who would turn us in and from the Guard. We shared MREs and granola bars, but even I could see that they wouldn't last for long between the five of us.

We were too afraid to make campfires at night, out of fear of being spotted outside such a populated area. So instead we bundled in the two fleece blankets that we thankfully had. Usually with Kate and I wrapped in one, Sam and Linc in another, and Luca sandwiched between us all. Luckily, spring in the south offered warm days and the temperatures didn't get too low on those nights. And Luca never complained.

Those days were spent hidden within the confines of the blooming trees around us. We watched cars carefully, spending time memorizing when the residents came and went. Lincoln liked to get up early, before the sun, to scout the area. Then he spent the days reading. He managed to pack a Bible and a few other treasured books into his bag. He and Sam always spent the afternoon together, near us, but alone in their own piece of the woods. Kate spent her mornings doing some sort of school work with Sam. Although I didn't see the point in this, Sam wanted to make certain that Kate didn't fall behind.

Luca helped Linc in the mornings and evenings watching for cars and neighborhood happenings. During the day he spent most of his time perched at the base of a tree reading, writing, and watching us all. His intensity made me uncomfortable and self-aware. I noticed on one of those days he sat fumbling with something in his hands, absent-mindedly. When I got close enough to see, I recognized the fabric number one patch, tattered and obviously pulled right off the bag that had been assigned to him in the gym.

On the third morning he asked if he could join me on my walk in the woods, which is how I spent my days there. When I had little to do, my mind raced with emotions and memories that I'd rather forget. I spent most of my day without speaking to any of them, pushing the shock induced nausea and panic as deep down within me as possible. I knew the others all gave me space in the wake of what had happened to my family. Walking the woods seemed to temporarily pacify the images of my parents and thoughts of Caleb when it seemed nothing else would. So, any company outside of myself was an invited distraction.

"You really don't mind being out here, do you?" He asked me as soon as we started walking. There was, I thought, admiration in his tone.

I hadn't thought about it until then, "Umm no. I guess I don't. Not really." I looked around me. Spring was in full bloom on the edges of every tree. Streams were moving in the distance, birds chirped like a chorus through the entirety of the woods around us, and the sun beamed through the shade above. It was comforting. Like light bursting into darkness.

"I spent a lot of time camping as a kid with my—with my family." It hurt to even mention them, "Did you camp at all? You seem pretty comfortable out here too." I tried to redirect, hoping he'd take over conversation and I wouldn't have to talk.

"Umm, yeah. I like being in the woods. The circumstances *could* be better. And I could do without mosquitos, but I'm thankful I'm with Lincoln and you girls," he glanced at me with color in his cheeks and continued on the path, "and I'm really thankful it isn't summer yet. Hopefully we'll be out of the woods by then." He was very sure of himself. Even if he did seem shy at times. He leaned down to pick up a rock and threw it deep into the woods, absentmindedly.

"And what about your family?" The words stumbled out of my mouth before I thought about what I was really asking. I was afraid. What if he had endured something like I had? I didn't think I could handle his mess in the midst of my own.

He hesitated and kept walking, but I noticed the tension rise in his face and his jaw tighten before he responded, "I don't really want to talk about it. If you don't mind." He went quiet again.

Back to the same old pensive Luca. And I felt ashamed. I didn't want anyone to talk about my family, did I? Why would I expect differently from him.

I tried to clear the air, "Right, um, yeah. Sorry." I looked away from him right as Kate ran into me, a welcome interruption.

"Hey, can I explore with you guys?!" She was excitable and a sweet distraction from the awkwardness that had risen between Luca and I.

"Of course you can, Katie," His countenance changed immediately, welcoming Kate and running ahead to look for lizards at the bottoms of tree trunks. The frustration I felt with the conversation magnified with how easily Luca seemed to be himself with everyone else. With Linc, Sam, and even Kate he was lighter somehow. With me, he was guarded. Our conversation seemed to only thicken the atmosphere between us. I didn't understand why it mattered to me, but it did. Kate joined him giddily, so I let them adventure alone and headed back to camp. That night we would move in on the Hall house.

Sam and Kate had left quickly when they realized their parents were not there, without grabbing much. Many of the Remnant families didn't prepare as well as ours had. Living on faith, or just refusing to accept that this reality could actually come to pass. They chose not to gather goods, food, supplies, or even to ready their kids for what may come. Sam and Kate's parents were some of them. As the day approached, many knew they were too late and had formulated quick plans. Sam was told to obey the Guard's orders. If her parents were not at home, they were to meet Linc at a pre-chosen spot and to stay together.

Even after days of watching the house I was skeptical and mostly afraid. The risk of getting caught was not worth what may be left there.

"I still don't think this is a good idea. What if it's being watched?" I argued.

Lincoln, though, didn't agree, "Why would they watch the

Hall house, Vala? The family isn't significant to the Remnant—No offense Sammy." He spoke to her apologetically, "They were just simple members. And we've been watching the street for days. No one has been here."

"Maybe our parents left something for us? A note, like Vala's mama," Kate said hopefully, and no one could bring themselves to correct or argue with her.

I tried to make them all see how dangerous this could be, "I don't think we should go in. It isn't safe. We should make a plan to get Caleb."

Even after watching for a few days from the woods, it didn't seem worth the risk, and fear governed my head and heart at this point. Sam stayed silent, not wanting to stir trouble between Linc and I. She looked between us all uncomfortably. And annoyance burned inside of me. Why did everything have to be so difficult? I wanted Sam to be on my side. Or to at least give her opinion.

Luca agreed with Linc too, "We have to go in, Vala. We won't do Caleb any good if we don't have food, clothes, or medical supplies. Besides, we don't even know where Caleb is. We have to get information. And we can't do that living in the woods."

His words hit like a punch to the gut. Information—I hadn't even thought of that. Who would possibly help us figure out where the Remnant youth were taken? Embarrassed by my own ignorance and frustrated with the lack of support, I silenced. I listened as the rest of the group agreed to wait at the edge of the Hall's neighborhood until nightfall, before splitting up to enter the house. Linc, Sam, and Luca would go to the house, while Kate and I waited at the tree line.

I wanted to be brave, to offer myself up to go to the house, but I couldn't. And it didn't make sense to anyhow. Sam was the best person to retrieve things from the house, for her and for Kate. She would grab a spare set of clothes for me from her own closet. There was no way that Lincoln would let her go without him and Luca would be useful if anything went wrong. Sam needed me to stay with Kate. To keep her safe. It gave me a job and security in the woods, so I agreed.

No one else would have been taken from this street. The Halls were the only members of the Remnant in their neighborhood. It gave me a small comfort knowing there wasn't a ton of destruction that we would meet here, in the wake of the previous week's events. I felt nervous as they left us on the tree line, but as it was past dusk now, so I knew they could move quickly and quietly as we waited. We watched as their silhouettes ran away from us toward the back of the houses, across the street from the Hall's home. All seemed well initially. Kate and I made small talk about the night air and discussed how we were thankful for a warmer evening. I knew Kate was afraid. And although I had known her since her birth, I was no substitute to the familiarity of Sam. But she never let on, chatting lightly like it was just another spring night, hanging out after school and supper.

Ten minutes passed. Then twenty. And then forty. What could they be doing in there for this amount of time?! I could sense that as the time passed, she knew too, that it was taking too long. At least, everything on the street had stayed still. Few cars drove into their garages for the night, and we could see lights through shaded windows, but little else happened.

Then, from the other entrance to the street, we saw movement. Three dark vans pulled up suddenly, but with their lights off. This had not happened on any of the evenings since we had been in the woods. They uniformly pulled into place, lining along the street as their dark shadows took up residence in the space that had been empty until now. The Guard had come. Although the darkness was closing in, we could see the shadows of figures beginning to walk along the street, in stealth. We had to act. We had to warn them.

All my feelings of unease and nerves joined with the adrenaline rushing through my body suddenly. I knew we'd only have a few minutes.

"Kate, feel like going for a little walk?" She nodded, understandingly and I spurted out directions, "Okay, I need you to stay as close to me as you can. Think you can do it?" She nodded again and grabbed my hand. We decided quickly which of the bags should be taken with us, but were forced to abandon a couple the others left behind. I noticed Luca's number one patch had fallen from one of the bags, so I put it in my pocket without thinking.

Kate and I jumped up from our spots silently and ran the tree line as far as we could to the house. We'd have to run through a neighbor's backyard and across the street to get to the Hall's. I prayed as we ran that we'd somehow make it there in time. Dogs on the street started barking, adding urgency to our strides. Were they detecting us or the darkened visitors from the other side of the street?

Running into the backyard across the street from the Hall's, I remembered that Jamie Fratz lived in the house next door. I had been there last summer for a pool party, Jamie's sweet sixteen. Our lives were so simple then. I had painstakingly picked out a bathing suit to wear for the occasion, finally settling on an emerald green one-piece. Mama said it flattered me and made my hair look more blonde.

It was the party of the year. Everyone I knew had been there. Even Luca showed up. We swam all afternoon, listening to music, and then spent the evening cheering on some of the guys in a pickup game of basketball. Jamie's parents finished the night off by surprising her with a car.

I could see the small navy sedan her parents gifted her with parked in the driveway as I crept alongside of the house. I was surprised, though, when I went around the corner and heard Kate greet Jamie quietly from behind the house.

"Hi Jamie," she spoke up innocently.

Stopping dead in my tracks, I immediately regretted not leaving Kate in the woods. "What are you doing?" I snapped, as I grabbed her by her backpack and pulled her close to me defensively.

Before Kate could respond, Jamie whispered reassuringly, "It's ok, Vala. I saw you running from the back." I hesitated. We didn't have time for this. And I wasn't sure we could trust anyone, even Jamie.

"I saw Sam go into the house," she whispered frantically, looking behind her as if someone would come out of the house at any moment. "My mom saw her too. And two people with her. Vala, she called the Guard," she admitted, looking horrified.

Even as she spoke I could sense the figures making their way up the street. Knowing they were getting closer and we hadn't warned the others in the house, I grew frantic, "Jamie, I have to warn them…please." I didn't know what I was asking, really, but she had been my friend and we had no other options at that point. Jamie had always been a bit shallow, but smarter than people gave her credit for.

She jumped into action, "I'll create a diversion on the right side of the neighbor's house. Run as soon as you get the chance!" You could hear the excitement, not without seriousness, in her voice.

I agreed quickly and grabbed Kate again to direct her to a hiding spot when Jamie stopped me and said coyly, "And Vala, there's a spare key under my passenger side door…" With that, she disappeared behind the backside of the house, her braided ponytail swinging behind her as she ran. I waited with Kate for the signal, bracing for the run across the street to the Hall's house.

It wasn't a minute later that we heard the sound of a window breaking loudly on the neighbor's back porch. Had she thrown a rock through? I felt myself smile for the first time in a week, grateful for her bravery. Grabbing Kate, I pulled her as fast as I could across the street when I knew the Guard was clear from view. Running to the left side of their house where a small porch opened to the kitchen door, we nearly ran straight into Linc.

He heard the commotion and ran to check. Anger, and I'm sure fear taking over him, he whispered at me, "What are you doing here, Vala? You were supposed to stay in the woods!"

I knew he was startled so I ignored the tone and explained as quickly as I could, "The Guard's here!"

He dragged us into the house to join Luca and Sam, who were rummaging through a kitchen pantry and the bottom of the kitchen cabinet, in what looked like a medical kit. I couldn't tell if the storm inside the house had been made by their search for supplies or by the Guard in search of them the week prior. But looking around I noticed photographs, coupons, and Mary Hall's grocery list still hanging from the face of the refrigerator. A picture Sam painted when we were little still hung in the place it always had over the kitchen window. For whatever reason, the Guard hadn't ransacked the place, the way they had our home.

We had minutes, if that, to get out. So when they looked up in surprise at Kate and I suddenly joining them, I blurted out, "We have to leave. NOW!"

Linc grabbed Sam, who was wearing a new sweatshirt retrieved from her room, and pulled her up by the arm, "The Guard's here, come on."

Luca shoved a last minute blanket into the bag he was holding and jumped up, meeting me at the entryway. "You ok? Did anyone see you?" He asked, concerned.

I nodded quickly, gathering myself, "I'm fine, but they definitely know we're here."

"How? How do we get out?" Sam cried, looking less put together than she had in a week. She pulled Kate close to herself protectively.

"I have a plan!" I surprised myself with the boldness that grew within me in the last few minutes. Pulling Luca by the arm towards the door, I quickly spit out directions, "Gather whatever you can and meet us at the side of the house in one minute."

Luca and I ran out and back to the side of the house where I had entered only a moment before, crouching low to the ground as we looked for any sign of the Guard's presence.

I knew they were there, but with no sign of them imminent, we had to cross. Luca asked no questions as I directed him to Jamie's passenger side door, and the spare key that she told me would be there. We made it quickly across the street, undetected by our hunters. But as Luca bent beneath the car to get the key, a motion-censored light turned on over the garage. And a group of three German Shepherds targeted him from a few houses down, across the street.

The Guard's pack.

I had heard rumors of trained dogs used by the Guard, but hadn't believed them really. It seemed like a weird conspiracy to scare us into submission. But they were real. The dogs were huge and aggressive, barking loudly as they attacked and one of them struck true to Luca's left arm and another at his side. Somehow managing to throw me the key over the car he yelled, "Get in!"

I jumped in, barely missing the dog that abandoned Luca and made its way quickly to my side. The brown beast slammed its body into the driver side door just as I closed it. Starting the car gave Luca a small window to kick one of the dogs hard in the face, as I instinctively opened his door and grabbed the back of his shirt. My Dad's shirt. And pulled him in as hard as I could. He was free of the dogs in one instant and I had the car in reverse across the street and in the side of the Hall's yard in the next. Panic stricken, I couldn't look at the wounds seeping from Luca's side and arm.

He was breathing heavily, out of step, and I knew from his deep, soft moans that the pain was tremendous. "Get us out of here, Vala," he managed to breathily get out in between groans.

The other three jumped in the car quickly, and I peeled out of the yard like a car chase I'd seen in a movie. I could see the lights of the dark vans behind me and knew we'd have to come up with a plan quickly. My mind raced. *Where could we go?* I ripped out of the neighborhood, swerving momentarily into the opposite lane as the back tires fishtailed behind us. I began to weave in and out of one lane of cars as Lincoln barked orders behind me. With every jerky movement I forced the car to make, Luca's low moans echoed from the passenger seat. Sam tried to assess the damage to Luca from the backseat, leaning over the middle partition, but we were driving too quickly and swerving too much to get a good look.

"We have to lose them! Get on the highway!" Linc yelled as I drove as fast as I could through the traffic. He directed me to a side highway in the city, covered with car dealerships. I was able to swing into a car lot, disguised by hundreds of sedans that looked exactly like Jamie's. By some means of grace, we watched as the vans passed us by, but knew it would not be long before the search steered back towards us. We waited. Luca was silent now and I thought maybe unconscious.

"Where can we go?" Sam asked aloud. The three of us started debating places we could dump the car while Kate watched us, her eyes bouncing from face to face in the darkness of the car.

"Do we know anyone we can trust to stay with?" Kate chimed in. She had been obviously terrified and silent up until that point.

We all answered, "No." A brief pause in our debate of whether we should go back to the woods or drive to a hotel.

"We can't use any money on a hotel, not when we don't know if we'll need it more later," Linc said, frustrated.

"We can't go back to the woods either," Sam chimed in, "they'll be looking for us near the house."

"We have to get somewhere clean to help Luca. And somewhere that we can stay for a while. He needs to be cleaned up." I felt sick thinking about how much blood he may have lost on our drive and as we sat wasting time in the parking lot. I allowed myself to glance at him and caught him hazily looking up at me, listening to the rest of us talk about him. He didn't say anything, but I was thankful he was at least conscious.

Linc popped up, excited, "Wait, what day is it?"

After some backtracking Sam determined that it was Friday. The *cafeteria day* and phase one of the Guard's plan had been the Thursday before. "Where could we go that is empty all weekend and no one would expect us to go?" Linc asked us all with a hint of mischief.

"Ah! Yes, Linc!" I saw where he was leading us and it was brilliant, "the school!"

The school would have a clean space, a few medical supplies, and we could stay all weekend without fear of anyone coming in. Who would think we'd go back to the very spot that they sent us away from? When we felt safe to make a move, I slowly pulled out from the lot, praying we'd avoid the Guard and that Luca's wounds were not as bad as they seemed.

Chapter 7

We decided to leave the car behind a strip mall parking lot, next to a dumpster. There didn't seem to be security cameras around, so hopefully we wouldn't be detected or followed. The strip mall was about a two-mile walk from the school and the closest area we could walk through a tree line undetected in. The walk took longer than it would have, considering we all carried packs filled with supplies from the house (but lacking the few left behind in the woods).

Kate and Sam walked ahead, scoping the area and making sure there was no movement at the school. Linc and I carried the weight of our bags and Luca, who was barely conscious, supported by his arms laid across our shoulders. I never really realized how tall and broad Luca really was, until we were dragging his body through the woods that night. He winced with every step we took and I felt guilty that my much smaller frame could not bear the weight and size of his well.

It was midnight before we reached the school. The parking lot was empty and quiet. Thankfully, the girls found an entryway from the back of the school gym. A small miracle to find an open, unlocked doorway. The path I had taken, only a week before with Caleb to leave the gym, was the same one we took to go back in. I imagined the weeds peeking from the cracks in the cement as we walked over them, towards the door. Sam and Kate settled into the gym, assessing the supplies we had and taking inventory of what could be helpful to Luca.

Linc and I dragged Luca to the boys locker room, leaning him sitting up against the milky, white tile of a shower. He groaned as we stripped him of the flannel, which amazingly survived the attack, minus tatters on the sleeve and a few blood stains. Linc held him in an upright position while I pulled the t-shirt off over his head. I tossed the shirts beside the shower and thought to myself that I could probably salvage both of the shirts later if I cleaned them by hand.

Wincing, Luca muttered something incoherently about, "... the first time a girl took my clothes off." Although I rolled my eyes a bit, I couldn't help but smile, thankful he had fully regained consciousness.

Lincoln bantered back, "It's not as exciting with me helping, man." And Luca actually laughed (and immediately groaned) at his response, putting his good hand over the wound on his waist.

Thankfully, the side injuries were not as bad as I anticipated. And somehow, the bleeding was less severe than I originally thought too. A deep bite left a wound just below his rib cage, which was the source of most of the bleeding there, but wasn't life threatening. His left hand, though, from the base of his thumb up to his forearm, took the brunt of the dogs' attack. The dogs had bitten and pulled and left little untouched. I cleaned as best as I could. First, with warm water. Then, with the peroxide Sam threw into her bag earlier at the house. Stepping back as Lincoln sat with him, I called out to Sam. Kate had since fallen asleep in between two bleacher steps while we worked on Luca.

"He's going to need stitches. He really needs a doctor," I muttered to her and to myself. I knew we couldn't seek one out, but didn't see how we'd get through this without medical help.

Sam looked worn down with weary, teary-eyes as she watched Linc and Luca sitting side by side on the shower floor, clearly exhausted. "We can't bring him anywhere else. We'll have to do it," she said. So sure of herself and with complete faith in us.

Faith, yes, but I also knew for a fact that Sam could not sew. Her mom sent jeans, dresses, and various quick hems to my house to be sewn over the years. My Mom was a craftsman at her machine, able to create something from nothing within an hour or so if she needed to. I was always amazed at the artistic hand she showed, even down to the stitching she chose on quilts and the gifts she'd make at the holidays for us all.

I could almost hear the humming sound of her machine and the warmth it created after being plugged in and used for hours at a time. And the cups of hot tea we'd share as she took small breaks. And she had insisted that I learn. First by hand, and then on the machine. I never had the patience to do much work on the sewing machine. It frustrated me to no end, really. I sewed more out of necessity and never with a perfectionistic eye. Hand stitching—I didn't know how I would bring myself to do it.

I found myself watching them all in slow motion, just as I had watched my family in the kitchen only a week before. Kate slept peacefully in the corner of the bleachers, covered by one of the small blankets we brought with us. Linc began to make sure we were secure within the walls of the gym, checking every door and pacing the brown gym floor, his sneakers squeaking occasionally as he walked. Luca had been left alone in the gym's locker room, asleep or passed out again. I wasn't sure.

Sam fluttered, as Mama had in the kitchen, gathering supplies for the task at hand. She was graceful and sure of herself, even in the midst of our situation. A thin pink scarf wrapped from the base of her skull to the top of her head resting in a small knot, as she often wore, holding her dark auburn hair out of her face.

The first week of kindergarten she gave me one similar, when a third grade boy told me I looked like a wet dog, after getting caught in the rain at recess.

"Now we can be twins," she had said, as she tied it into my dirty-blonde hair. I wore the scarf every day for a year and we had been best friends ever since. Even then, she took care of me. She set me at ease.

A week before, I was scolding Caleb for the way his bedroom smelled like sweat and socks. I teased friends at lunch about getting married to a lowly freshman. I was studying, reading, hanging out with friends, planning for prom, arguing with my parents about school and curfews—and now I was on the run. An orphan. Sleeping in the woods. I was a car thief, hiding out in the school gym, and mentally prepping myself to sew into a guy's arm. How had this become my reality?

I went to check on Luca in the locker room as the others worked. Asleep on the white tiles of one of the showers, he had propped himself up in a corner. I watched the steady movement of his chest as he took deep breaths, in and out.

"It's freezing in here," I whispered to myself, looking for something I could cover his bare chest with.

"I feel fine," he muttered.

"Oh, I'm sorry. I didn't mean to wake you." I fumbled around in a bag looking for something and when I couldn't find a blanket I settled on the flannel again. Draping it over his chest, I could feel that he was cold. "Liar," I laughed as I brought the shirt up under his chin.

He managed a smile at me, "I've got to keep up my tough guy rep for the ladies."

"Well, I'll tell you one thing, Luca Alexis, you're much more likable after a good dog attack." He sighed and nodded at me, a small smile still lingering across his face.

I sort of meant it. Luca was always so serious when we interacted. Even that morning he managed to relax for only a few minutes while we walked through the woods, only to go cold again when I mentioned his family. Granted, we had only spoken a handful of times since he moved to our town. Maybe he was shy, or just quiet tempered, but he always seemed more mature than any of the other boys we went to school with. Even more so than Lincoln. He followed Linc around for the past two years. Linc's friends became his acquaintances, but only Linc really knew him. He rarely included himself into our conversations and I wasn't sure that he really interacted with anyone aside from Linc, and maybe Brian Acworth, who they played basketball with weekly.

"We have to stitch up your arm and your waist." I broke the news as he readjusted his spot on the slick tile.

"I know." He was somber again, but calm, "I heard you and Sam before. Are you going to do it?" I gave a quick nod. Wishing I didn't have to.

"Ok then," he slumped back down and put his good hand on his abdomen, "I'll just wait here until you're ready,"

Lincoln joined Sam in the hunt for the tools I needed. They managed to find a needle in the front office and a couple packs of floss in various teachers' desks. Linc remembered learning in Scouts that floss could be used for field stitching, so we made the best of what we had. Pain relievers, gauze, alcohol and peroxide they'd gotten from the house for sterilizing, and tape they found with relative ease in the nurse's office as well.

Sam gave Luca the pain relievers right away and a refilled bottle of water. "Drink it all, okay. You need to hydrate," she mothered him as she did us all, placing her hand gently on his bare shoulder as she spoke.

He nodded compliantly, "I will, Sam. Thank you."

She gave him a smile, patted him on the shoulder and turned to me, "Vala, do you need anything else?"

I gave our makeshift workstation a glance, as if I somehow had the knowledge of everything I would need for the task, and sighed, "I think I have everything I need."

At that she grabbed Linc's hand and led him towards the gym floor, "We're gonna let you work, then."

I was surprised at Luca's reaction to me as I sat down to prep his arm, now wide awake and clearly feeling the full effects of the attack. "I trust you, Vala," he said, so earnestly.

"Really?" I breathlessly asked, and then reminded him, "You barely know me if you think about it. I'm not sure I'm feeling too confident about it." I felt kind of guilty immediately and wished I thought more before I spoke. We all had been through so much together over the course of the past week, it felt wrong to show him so little care. Even if it was mostly true.

I stumbled, trying to find a way to recover and help encourage him somehow, when he laid his uninjured hand over mine, just as he had done in the woods only a week before. "Vala," he looked directly at me now, "I know you can do this."

I sighed with nervousness. "I hope you like peppermint," I said shakily, showing off the first container of floss. I remembered the patch I shoved into my pocket back in the woods and handed it over to him. "Oh, I found this earlier. I recognized it from that day in the gym."

"Oh. Yeah, thanks for that," He took it in his good hand timidly, "It must have fallen out of my pocket." He clenched the patch and looked at his other hand, "Alright, I'm ready when you are."

I felt unsteady, but began to work as soon as we felt the area was as clean and prepped as it could be. Lincoln and Sam decided to rest, agreeing to take watch over the school and over Luca as soon as I completed my work.

It took everything. Everything. Not to gag my way through the first couple of stitches. I decided to start with his abdomen. It was not as gruesome as his hand and would only require a few stitches to close. I knew Luca had to be in utter agony with every pierce of the needle into the open skin, but he stayed steady. He talked to me about his first summer in our town. About the time he spent with Brian and Lincoln, playing basketball and swimming in the lake that summer. He moved from up north a few hours when his Dad took a job in the middle of his high school career. Moving, he said, was hard on his family life, but strengthened his faith.

I was grateful for the distraction that conversation brought from the work of my hands and surprised by how much he was divulging to me. It was the most relaxed Luca had ever been around me. And his calmness steadied my nerves.

It was rare for me to hear anyone my age, much less a guy, speaking so openly about his faith and the challenges he had faced. Linc and Brian were stabilizers in his life, pointing him to the truth when he felt discouraged. I could hear the admiration in his voice as he spoke about them. And I found myself admiring him more as he spoke. Softly. Casually. He took deep breaths between every few words.

It took at least an hour to finish. I hoped he wouldn't hate me later for the gnarly scars I was sure would develop, but I was so thankful to see the wounds closed now and no longer seeping. His words became fuzzier as I cleaned his forearm again. Luca had managed to keep the conversation and my attention the entire time, until he eventually quieted and passed out. From pain or exhaustion, I wasn't sure. I cleaned him, checked the wound on his side once more and cleaned that area too, as gently as I could. He stirred a few times, but never fully woke up. I was clinical and focused, taking care not to be over abrasive and looking at his chest and arms as merely the palette or the table in which I had to work— until I finished.

When I finally took a step back, I allowed myself to breathe more fully. Then, I couldn't help but notice him. Not his wounds, but him. Luca was eighteen, a year older than Sam and I. But he didn't look like a boy anymore. His arms and chest were filled out with muscle, a slight farmers tan framing them. While Linc was lanky and slim, Luca was broad-shouldered, tall, and strong.

I studied his breath moving his chest up and down and the way his lips opened slightly as he slept. He was filthy from our week in the woods. His brown hair, disheveled and wavy, fell slightly across his forehead. The jeans hugging his lower waist and his gray tennis shoes had seen better days. Embarrassed at my unexpected gaze, I felt my cheeks go warm and my heart fluttering in my chest. Thankful no one had seen, I left him there in the locker room to retrieve Lincoln and Sam for their shift.

I hated to wake Linc and Sam, but felt my own exhaustion taking over. Finding them in the gym below the bleachers where Kate slept, they looked completely at peace. They lied next to each other, Lincoln on his back stretched out. One arm folded beneath his own head while the other acted as a pillow for Sam, who curled towards him. Small throw blankets, retrieved from the Hall house, covered Sam and Kate. Sam shifted and Linc turned to his side, drawing her in closer with his free arm. I felt like an intruder to their intimacy, as innocent as it was.

Hesitating, but knowing I wouldn't make it much longer I gently shook Linc's shoulder. "Linc, I need you to take your watch," I whispered, but Sam woke, a haze over her eyes and a gentle smile on her face.

"You must be so tired, Vala," she smiled at me, holding her hand out for mine, "we'll take it from here."

They both slowly sat up, passing the blanket on to me, and made their way to the entrance to the locker room. They'd stand post to watch over us in the gym and to keep an eye on the sleeping patient. I drifted easily off to sleep, wedging myself in between the bleacher seats, thoughtless and numb to everything that had transpired. Emptied.

Chapter 8

WE WERE RUNNING THROUGH THE WOODS AGAIN. LIGHTHEARTED and free. I was warm with morning sunlight. I could see Caleb just in front of me. I could stretch my arm out and touch him if he just slowed down a bit. The sun flashed through the trees, casting shadows over his back as he passed under them, laughing for me to catch up. I tried. I tried and willed my feet to pass faster beneath me, but despite my want I can't. He slipped behind a tree. Gone. He was just—Gone. Turning in circles beneath the pines I felt frantic. My breath came faster and faster now. Panic set in. Where could he have gone so quickly?

And then… darkness. I was alone in the woods again. Next to the oak covered in kudzu, by the hole. I couldn't see in the darkness, but I knew Daddy lay nearby, cold and quiet. I sunk beneath the tree and wrapped my cold arms around my knees.

And I could hear Mama's voice call out to me from the woods, "Find him Vala. Find Caleb…. Find Micah." Her voice didn't bring *me comfort in the woods though, it scared me. Relentlessly, she repeated it, over and over again. I could see her again, there on the floor of our house, cradling her stomach, "Find him."*

Afraid. Desperate to leave the woods and to be free of her pleas I cupped my filthy, shaking hands over my ears to drown her out. In darkness, I rocked my body back and forth and prayed for release.

I woke to find a small hand in mine, Kate comforting me from the depth of my nightmare. She said nothing and only smiled lightly, nodding and giving my hand a squeeze before getting up and leaving me on the bleachers. Covered in cold sweat and shaking, I wasn't surprised to find myself out of breath and anxious as I looked around the gym quickly. I jumped up and made myself busy to avoid the eyes of anyone who may have seen me, taking longer than necessary to fold up my blanket.

In reality, none of them watched me. Kate had gone to join Linc, who was digging out protein bars for our breakfast in one of the packs. He teased her, holding a bar out of reach until after stepping on her tippy toes, she jumped as high as she could to grab it. I couldn't see Luca and Sam from my quick overview. The sun was bursting its light and warmth through the windows at the top of the gym, a welcome contrast to the darkness of my nightmare.

"Where's Sam?" I asked aloud, as I took the awkward steps down from my bed on the bleachers.

Linc gestured his head toward the locker room, "She's just keeping Luca company. He's doing much better this morning. You did a good job, Vala." He smiled and relief shown across his face. I thanked him for the protein bar he tossed to me and made my way to the locker room, still feeling a bit unsettled.

Luca clearly felt better. He was sitting up, talking animatedly about something with Sam. He used his uninjured hand to tell a story as his knee propped up his bad hand. I liked the way he made her laugh. She sat cross-legged, listening undistractedly to him. He wore the flannel again, buttoned halfway up his chest. I had never seen him so unhindered and relaxed. It was like I was seeing more and more of who Luca really was. He and Sam both snacked on protein bars and sat with ease together. They knew each other relatively well, with Linc connecting them over the last two years.

Noticing me at the doorway, their conversation paused. Sam greeted me with a casual wave, "Mornin' Vala." I never understood how Sam could stay so light-hearted in the midst of any situation. Her gentleness set me at ease, always this constant force of positivity in our group. "Did you sleep ok?"

"I did," I answered. It wasn't a lie. I felt rested. Even if that rest ended with the sound of Mama crying out to me in the darkness. "You look much better today," I walked toward them, taking her greeting as an invitation to join them.

"Thanks for last night, Vala. I know what you did wasn't easy," Luca looked earnestly at me.

"Ha!" I laughed out loud as I took a place beside Sam, "My job was a breeze compared to yours. Wait to thank me until after we see what the scar looks like."

"Ya know, girls are into scars, Luca. You've got an air of mystery now," Lincoln and Kate had snuck in behind us. Kate giggled as she came in.

Rolling her eyes, Sam laughed, "And how would *you* know, babe?!" She stretched out her hand for Linc to sit with her. Kate followed suit.

I felt so relaxed for the first time since this misadventure had started. We sat around Luca, debating the intricacies of the perfect protein bar flavor. It was all so normal. And also so surreal. After morning pleasantries, teasing Kate for snoring (although she didn't), and talking over shower schedules, we took time to pray. Placing our hands on Luca, we prayed specifically for his healing. For our families, wherever they may be. For safety, security, and for freedom. We were thankful for our provisions, for Jamie's selflessness the night before, for a place to sleep, the perfectly flavored bars in our bellies, and for each other. But most of all, we were thankful knowing there was so much more than this life offered and that our hope rested in the Savior who had already come and won the battle for us. Praying was a ritual we had fought for, one our parents had instilled in us and some had died for. It was something we tried to do each morning since we had come together. As a family of sorts.

The weekend in the gym was the regeneration we needed. Saturday was spent taking showers to wash off the filth from the week's events. We rinsed clothes, as mine and Luca's in particular were soiled with blood. And we rested. Kate napped all afternoon. Lincoln played basketball, with Luca watching and giving him friendly advice nearby. Sam, always the mother hen, cleaned up our area and made sure we had a plan for the supplies we had gathered together.

I checked Luca's wounds and rebandaged with the spool of gauze we had. He was quiet, but seemed comfortable, no longer trying to distract me as he had the night before. I could feel his eyes studying my face as I inspected and I tried not to linger too long at his side. Still unhinged a bit by the way my stomach fluttered suddenly when my fingers brushed his skin, I removed his bandages and worked quickly. Our new familiarity with each other didn't make me feel any less awkward to be alone with him.

By all accounts the injuries looked good. Sam had the foresight to grab untaken antibiotics from her house the night before and we started Luca on a regimen of one of the leftover bottles and more pain relievers, hoping they would prevent any infection that might grow. The stitches were far from perfect and would definitely leave scars, but they were doing their job. Satisfied, I stood quickly, "You're gonna make it."

He smiled at me from his spot on the floor, "Thanks Doc. I'm sure you've got a bright future in medicine." He teased. And I felt a little more at ease, even if a little unsteady. "Thank you again for grabbing the patch for me," he motioned to where it lay beside his bag.

"Why did you do it? Keep it, I mean. I left mine at the house," I confessed, quietly. I wanted no token of my so called rebellion against the government.

"It's a reminder, I guess." He pushed the patch around the floor gently with his finger.

"Of what you've lost?"

He looked up with conviction and answered simply, "Of what I've gained."

It felt so strange to have this new found friendship with Luca. Of course we had been at parties together and spent time with mutual friends over the past two years, but we rarely spoke before the night they found me in the woods. Looking back, I even felt like Luca maybe avoided me at times. Now I trusted him and the others with my life. The past week bound us deeply together.

We laughed a lot that day. Playing house and pretending we could stay in the gym forever was a happy distraction from reality. The gym felt safe. Familiar. Caleb plagued the back of my mind and I knew that this, obviously, could not be home. Not without him. And not in this place.

We prayed again at dinner and shared another MRE of chicken and rice, with dehydrated mushrooms and carrots. Everyone seemed satisfied and we all slept in the gym without a watchman that night. Confident in the security of its warm walls.

Sunday brought rain and readiness. We knew our weekend of peace would come to an end. After our morning ritual of praying together and reading scripture, we all took long hot showers, not knowing when we'd have access to that luxury again.

That morning we read from the gospel of Matthew which instructed believers to, *Love your enemies and pray for those who persecute you...*

I recited those words over and over again in my head, letting them wash over me as the gym shower's hot water slowly dwindled. *How could I possibly love those who had forced us from our homes? How could I love the neighbors who wouldn't stand up for us? Who* believed we were rebels. How could I pray for the men who had made me an orphan? And how could Jesus ask this of his followers? Of me...

The afternoon was spent discussing our next move. We had to get information on where Caleb could have possibly been taken. Lincoln heard rumors of camps in the mountains up north. It would be at least a three to four hour drive, but we had no car. Should we try to hitchhike? Steal a car? Buy one?

Luca had saved money over the past four summers, initially for a college fund, working at a tree cutting service over the summers. Then he worked small jobs for his Dad. I felt so guilty even considering using his hard earned money, money he had built dreams upon, to chase Caleb. And we didn't even know where he was.

"The money doesn't matter anymore. I can't use it for school anyways," he argued with us, sacrificing up his savings for our betterment.

"How would we even go about buying a car without being taken?" Sam asked. She looked towards Linc, but Luca answered first.

"We're paying in cash. It's not like we're trying to get a loan, Sam. We'll make sure it's safe." He was so eager to help and reasoned with us, "I wouldn't be recognized regardless. Not many people in town really know who I am. I could be in and out of the dealership in a couple of hours." He looked to me and said, "I really want to do this. For Caleb."

I stayed silent. I didn't feel right offering up an opinion when it felt so self-servicing to my own wants. I had to find Caleb. I didn't want to use Luca's money, but ultimately I would do whatever was necessary. I had my own cash, but it was nowhere near what we needed. I was grateful for his willingness.

Lincoln finally spoke up and agreed with Luca, although reluctantly at first,

"I think he's right. We needed a plan and this is the best

we've come up with," he looked at Sam and Kate, "We can't keep trekking through the woods to nowhere. It's not safe. And it's not getting us any closer to Caleb."

Turning back to Luca and I he went on, "Luca, you'll have to go alone. Too many people know the girls and I in town." Lincoln seemed reluctant, but Luca nodded in agreement.

We all agreed that despite the means, having access to a car would change our situation dramatically. Monday morning, before the sun rose, we would leave the security of our gym again and begin the walk to a local dealer. The rest of us would wait in hiding while Luca made the deal and then we could head north, in the direction of the rumored internment camps.

The day passed quickly. The gym darkened and grew chilly as the sun went down, and as the night grew closer I dreaded the next day. The gym had provided protection we hadn't had in weeks. We had slept, showered, laughed—for two days it had been home. We were safe. Now we were going back into the wilderness, facing countless unknowns.

That evening, Linc and Luca spent most of their time whispering together plans for the next day as Sam, Kate, and I set to work on packing our belongings. Shoving everything we could into backpacks, and layering on the little clothing that we owned was a quick job. As we finished and cleaned up the gym a bit from our time there, Kate and Sam found their way to each other on the bleachers and shared a blanket for bed. I stole a glance at the guys, still huddled together in discussion and tried to read their faces. Were they arguing? Linc looked concerned and Luca, dismissive. I couldn't resist the urge to hear what they were saying and jumped up to join them.

"Hey guys, what's going on over here?" I whispered, trying to lighten the mood and shove my way into their conversation. I awkwardly tripped the tip of my converse across the basketball court floor, squeaking it loudly as I stumbled over.

Their faces changed immediately.

Linc reassured me quickly, laughing a bit at my fumbling, "Oh nothing, we're just settling plans for tomorrow." Luca, though, looked awkward about my sudden interruption. Uncomfortable even. It was a far cry from his behavior towards me the previous day.

Avoiding my eyes he mumbled something about needing rest and patted Linc on the back with his good hand. He said goodnight abruptly to us both and made his way to the spot on the bleachers he slept on the previous night. It felt like I had walked into an argument or a secret. Both made me nervous.

I grabbed Lincoln's arm as he turned to walk towards the bleachers too, "Seriously, Linc, what's going on?! Am I missing something?"

"It's nothing. I was just reminding him that he can't be recognized. There's nothing to worry about though, okay?"

I replied quickly, so he couldn't walk away from me, "But, Luca said no one would recognize him in town. He seemed pretty sure. Why are you so worried? Who are you worried about seeing him?"

He hesitated and I felt like he wanted to tell me what they had spoken about, but instead after a pause, he ended with, "You just never know. We're taking a big risk. I just want to make sure he's safe. That's all." Half smiling and feigning a yawn, he rubbed his hands through is thick hair and turned towards the bleachers, "I'm gonna get some rest before tomorrow. You should too, Vala. 'Night."

He made his way to where the girls had laid down, adjusting the blanket over Kate and settling down next to Sam. I was left there, alone and worried.

Lincoln, Sam, and Kate were piled together on the bleachers, and I could see my dad's flannel draped across Luca's body, with his back to us all. I laid awake, restless that night. Nerves plagued me thinking of the next day, of the exchange between Linc and Luca, and mostly I dreaded the unknown road ahead of us.

Chapter 9

We woke the next morning, long before the sun would rise and before students would arrive. Reluctantly and mostly silent, we left the safety of the gym. It was bizarre knowing that our friends, people we had spent each day with since elementary school, but who felt like strangers now, would be coming into the place that had been our safe haven for a short time. Would they run laps around the gym floor, as we had so many times before? Would they suspect someone had been there? Our lives were so very different from theirs now.

We followed our steps back through the cracking parking lot to the woods and began the hike towards town. Driving on the highway, it would have taken only about twenty minutes to get to the cash-only car dealership Linc and Luca knew about. Walking through the woods, so as not to be seen, would take much longer. Luca would have to go to an ATM to get the rest of his cash. We prayed there'd be one nearby the lot.

The morning was mostly quiet. Mist covered the forest floor from the weekend of rain and it looked as if it would rain more before the day was through. The early May morning proved to be cooler than most. Walking through the pines, hickory trees, and freshly risen wildflowers as the sun rose and broke through a cloudy morning sky, was almost enough to make me forget our present situation. With the hood of my sweatshirt over my head and the sleeves grasped tightly over my hands, I wrapped myself up in its warmth and the morning's beauty. The silence between us was unusual and yet, refreshing. I prayed silently and hung behind to watch the others walk ahead, soaking in the solitude.

I always had an appreciation for the outdoors. Daddy and Mama took Caleb and I hiking up north whenever we had breaks from school. We'd wake up early, not unlike that morning, to watch the sun rise over a ridge. Sometimes Dad would lead us in a devotional when we made it to the top or Mama would sing. Other times we were silent, like now, taking in the beauty that God had made. We packed lunches for day trips, carried tents on our backs for overnights, and even went for weekend getaways now and then.

I loved the peace of the woods, hearing a stream nearby without quite being able to see it. Discovering a new path, rock, or treasure along the way. It almost felt like one of those days on this morning. Peace. Quiet. The trickle of raindrops falling off of leaves above us. A song Mama sang to us on those trips echoed through my thoughts,

> *In the morning, when I rise.*
> *In the morning, when I rise.*
> *In the morning, when I rise.*
> *Give me Jesus.*
> *You can have, all this world, but give me Jesus.*

I imagined her voice, walking beside me that morning, worshiping in the expanse of the woods.

Sam and Linc were in the front, holding hands as if they were on a leisurely walk together. Sam's hair, as always, was pulled up with a pink bandana. Linc's favorite red baseball hat covered the top of his head, with his dark hair just slightly peeking through the back strap. I had seen him with that hat on more than with it off. The familiarity of their steps together was comforting to watch. Linc, always leading, held her hand and helped her along over stumps and around holes.

They were inseparable, their hands and fingers weaving in and out of each other as they walked the path. Although his tall, lanky body created an unbalance with her much shorter frame, they had a rhythm together that seemed so effortless. They talked easily as they walked, and she giggled a few times, although I couldn't tell from my distance and past their quiet words, what he had said to make her laugh.

Kate followed closely behind Sam, as always. She picked dandelions off of the forest floor as we went, fumbling with them a bit as we walked. Eventually she placed a crown of them on her head, with her long auburn hair flowing behind her. I loved her innocence and also her strength. She was ten and had already comforted me on multiple occasions over the week we spent so closely together. She skipped and stumbled, and danced around the woods as we made our way to our destination. She absentmindedly watched the tops of trees looking for birds and their trunks for lizards and even tried to start a conversation with Luca.

Luca, however, was less lighthearted than I had seen him in a few days. His stride was stern and direct. He was tense. And he seemed to have reveled in the silence too. He wore jeans and the blue and black flannel again, a staple I rarely saw him without since gifting it to him in the woods on the first night. Walking directly in front of me, he generally avoided all of us that morning. Although, no one could really resist Kate. Especially with that yellow crown of wildflowers on her head.

I watched him smirk at her as she floated in a circle around him, obviously sensing he needed cheering up. She took three steps to one of his, looking like a fairy girl walking beside him.

"Do you like my crown, Luca?" She looked up at him proudly.

"I do," he answered, simply.

"Sammy and Vala taught me to make flower crowns when I was seven. Now I'm *really* good at making them. I can make one for you if you want? I mean, they are for girls, but you could wear one." She was chatting on and on without really needing a reply from him along the way, "I like to wear them as necklaces too, if you have the right flowers. I think I'll make one of those for you."

He smirked, "That'd be great, Kate."

"Katie girl, come here," Sam called out to her, interrupting her mostly one-sided conversation with Luca. Kate ran to meet Sam and Linc up ahead, and took the water bottle Sam offered her.

I took the opening and caught up to Luca, breaking the previous silence between us, "So, what color crown will you wear?"

He smiled, "I think I'm gonna just have to see what she brings me. You should ask for one too."

I was relieved with his ease and thought maybe I had imagined his earlier mood. "How are you feeling today?" I gestured to his bandages.

Rubbing his abdomen slightly he said, "My stomach feels fine, just a little itchy now. My arm still hurts, but I'm sure it will take some time."

"Itchy, do you think it's infected?" I tried to hide the worry in my voice and insisted he let me look quickly. What could I do really? Nothing. But I felt responsible, somehow, for his wellbeing and his wounds.

Pausing and letting the others walk ahead a bit, he pulled up the stomach bandage slightly. It didn't look overly red or irritated. It was healing, thankfully. I made sure not to touch him while inspecting the wounds, as I had the days before. My unease around him had stirred something within me that I had never felt before.

Luca made me nervous. Being around him, alone, made me feel fluttery. I found myself wanting to talk to him, but then not knowing what I would say when I actually did. These wound inspections were the best of both worlds. I rested his wounded hand upright in mine. His arm, although healing, looked rough. It was red and inflamed, but really no more than I expected. The stitches looked clean and like they were holding. We would need to cut them out at the end of the week. A thought I pushed from my mind.

"Satisfied?" He asked, with a small smile, looking down at me in close proximity.

I felt flustered again and dropped his hand quickly, but replied, "I suppose. Don't forget to take those antibiotics, ok?" I paused, wanting to sound less like his doctor, "I'm really glad you had a couple of days to rest." He nodded and we walked again silently for a few minutes.

In an effort to break the quiet again I asked, "Do you feel nervous about today?"

I did.

"No," he responded quickly, without offering anything more.

"Was everything okay last night? Between you and Lincoln, I mean. You seemed, I don't know, kind of worried." He seemed irritated really, but I thought better of saying it outright.

I clearly caught him off guard, but he managed to muster up, "Everything's fine. We were just making plans for today."

"Yeah that's what Linc said too." That was all I was going to get out of him about that. "Sorry if I was rude to interrupt. You just seemed to be…"

He stopped me, "You weren't rude. Not at all. I was just—just thinking a lot about what we need to do. What I need to do, today. Sorry to worry you."

He added, reassuringly, "Everything's 'gonna be fine." I nodded with understanding and we walked for a bit beside each other. I wanted to keep talking to him, but floundered for topics. Why did I feel so nervous?

"Luca, ummm… where did you go after the school that day?" I knew that he knew which day I was talking about and I felt weird immediately for bringing it up.

"I went to Linc's place. We made a plan together about a year ago. He said goodbye to Sam. I mean, we saw you in the gym, right? And then we drove—I mean…"

I interrupted before he could retract anything and the air between us abruptly changed. "You—you drove? You drove what?" I was surprised by his accidental admission. And then surprise quickly grew to anger as realization entered my thoughts. "You've had access to a car all this time?!"

My voice was irritated and louder than it had been. I knew it caught the attention of the others ahead of us, as I saw them all pause, but I didn't care. I suddenly felt stupid, realizing I knew Luca drove a black sedan. I didn't know what kind it was exactly, but I'd seen him in it a few times.

"What in the world are we doing here, then?" I could see Lincoln catching Sam's arm to stop her from interrupting, which made me more irritated. Did they all know that Luca had a car?

Luca sighed, "Yeah, but we can't use my car, Vala. We left it at Linc's and it isn't safe to go back there."

"Why? Is this what you guys were whispering about last night? Luca, we don't have to use your savings now! Let's just make a plan to go get the car."

He picked up his pace, leaving me behind and shaking his head. "Leave it alone, Vala. We can't."

After hesitating for a second, another realization came to my mind, "Wait, why didn't you go to your own house after we were sent home?" I took a few steps to catch up with him, "And you live in the same neighborhood as Linc, right? We can go back, like we did to Sam's. Let's watch for a few days and then pick up the car."

I looked for backup from the other three, but no one seemed to agree with me.

Sam spoke up, but not for me, "It would be too dangerous, Vala. It has to be this way." She walked towards me a few steps. She was trying to reassure me, but it felt like she knew something I didn't.

Confused and frustrated, I ignored her, "Why didn't you go home, Luca? I mean, don't you have a family wondering where you are?" I grabbed his shirt sleeve to make him stop and listen to me. To give me some sort of answer. "Where are *your* parents?"

The last question stung as it left my throat. I couldn't let it go. We were walking *again*, through the woods exhausted, and wet now from grass and humid air. Luca had homemade floss stitches in his arm and abdomen, and we were carrying all of our belongings on our backs. Yet, all of this time we could have had a car. And I was bothered that I suddenly realized I didn't know what happened to him that day. Why wouldn't he go to his own home?

"I just didn't, ok!?" He was defensive, now, "Forget about the car. It's not happening. We have to keep going if we are going to make it there this morning." He looked towards the others to start walking again. They turned, though reluctantly, and I noticed Sam looked especially pained to turn away from me. Linc wrapped his hand around her waist and pushed her forward, with Kate holding her hand at her side.

I tried to push past Luca, but he grabbed my hand as I did, "Vala, I'm sorry I didn't tell you. It's—it's just kind of complicated." Less defensive, he seemed contrite and even a little worried. "I'm sorry. I really am. I just need you to trust me, okay? We can't use my car. But let me do this for you and the others— and for Caleb. I don't care about the money." He stared into my eyes, earnestly searching for some sign that I would understand.

I didn't.

I ripped my hand from his, and walked past, retorting, "Yeah, it's complicated. I couldn't possibly understand." I hated that they all had kept this from me. I felt stupid. They had seen my family cut down. They found me broken down in a literal hole, and yet, they still didn't trust me because *It's kind of complicated.* And I was frustrated with myself. I felt this sudden comradery with Luca, like we were connected through the weekend's events. But maybe I had imagined it if he wasn't willing to tell me what I thought were some pretty straight forward questions. I felt foolish.

I stayed quiet the rest of the morning, walking between them all. I could sense Luca behind me, but wouldn't allow him to catch up. We made it to a point in the woods, just before the edge of the highway around eleven a.m. We were adjacent to the car dealership, which was just down the road. An ATM could be seen in the front of the building, a welcome blessing after the frustrating morning. The dealership, *Donnie's Rides* looked sketchy, with a flashing *Open* sign and a *No Questions Asked* sign barely glowing below it, but apparently it was our only option.

The mood was tense again. Luca looked like a damp dog, saved from a storm after running away. His demeanor changed even from earlier in the morning. He avoided me completely and instead talked to Lincoln one more time. I felt twinges of guilt at the way I attacked him, particularly in regards to his family, but righteous anger ruled. Why were they keeping things from me?

We prayed together for Luca's safety and he stumbled off towards the lot of cars just as it began to rain again. The four of us took cover under a group of low hanging tree limbs while we waited. They sheltered us a bit, but we were soaked within an hour. The smell of rain hitting the kudzu-covered ground filled the space around us. Thankfully, it was too early in the season for a real southern storm, but the summer would bring with it rising temperatures and thunder storms. We would not want to be hidden under the shelter of these trees for them. We did need a car. We needed permanent shelter. And while I didn't understand the reasoning or the secretive nature of Luca's own car, this plan made the most sense right now.

The other three made small talk and eventually took to quizzing Kate on basic math questions. I took solace in silence and willed myself to pray. I knew I was being petty and overreacting, but I couldn't help feeling that they were all keeping something from me. Maybe not Kate, but the other three were. It was hard to shake off. In my heart, I wanted them to know I was angry, but in my spirit, I knew I'd have to forgive them and move on.

The rain grew relentless as the afternoon progressed, and I started to grow nervous as time passed. Fear plagued me at times like this and I felt like everyone else seemed so calm. I imagined Caleb telling me to *chill out*, or Mama's stroke against my cheek telling me everything would be okay. But would things ever be okay again?

Eventually, Linc and I decided to check Luca's progress from the edge of the woods after three hours had passed. There we saw three black SUVs blocking the entrances and exits to the lot. The Guard. Not only were they surrounding the lot, but men in suits could be seen around the entire perimeter, searching on foot. I felt sick with fear. They had found us again. Did they have Luca? How long before they came across the little highway to our spot in the woods. I couldn't believe we had been so stupid. Linc, strangely calm, grabbed my arm and gestured for me to move quickly behind the tree line again.

I began muttering frantically "What are we going to do?! We have to get him. Linc, we've got to run! Let's go tell the gir—" He put his hand over my mouth and his other around the back of my head and stared at me more seriously than he ever had. His dark brown eyes stared into mine with urgency and authority.

"Vala, Luca and I knew this was a possibility. We made a plan. They wouldn't be searching if they had him, right? You have to calm down and we have to get back to Sam and Kate, now. And quietly." My heart pounding through my chest. I nodded in agreement, and only then did Linc release me.

We ran back to the girls, who were still huddled beneath the tree. They read the look on our faces immediately and jumped up. Kate looked terrified. I held her close, in front of me, while Linc explained everything to them. We were supposed to meet Luca, if he got away, at a rest stop three exits north off the highway. It would be dark soon, darker than it was even now with the rain. We would have to run.

There's an exhaustion that sets in, when you're mentally and physically worn. When you're soaked to the bone with southern, spring rain and dragging wet jeans and tennis shoes. I called it *amusement park legs*. That absolute dead-tired feeling after a full day at an amusement park and you're positive your legs won't carry you a single step further. But they do. My gray converse were soaked with red clay and soil, and every inch of me hurt, but I ran the three miles as fast as my legs would step in front of the other. I felt like we were in slow motion. Linc was leading us through the darkening woods again. Sam, Kate, and I did everything we could to keep up, with the sound of cars on the highway nearby.

Linc and I made it to the rest stop first. Sam had to stay back with Kate who couldn't keep up with Linc's strides. After looking around the perimeter, we ran to the rest stop. It was just past rush hour, and there were no cars in the parking lot, and thankfully no members of the Guard this far north, yet. Lincoln ran up to the front, while I made my way around the back.

And then I saw him, jogging slightly from the tree line behind the rest stop.

"Luca!" I ran towards him and fell into his arms. I heard him wince slightly at the sheer force of my body hitting his. My head cradled against his rain soaked chest by his arms wrapped around me and I felt deeply out of breath, with exhaustion and relief.

"I'm okay. I'm okay, Vala." He kept repeating it, reassuring me, "It's okay."

"I'm so sorry. It was none of my business. Earlier today. I—I'm really sorry." I couldn't believe we found him. My hands clung to the front of his shirt, my dad's old flannel shirt, and I realized how great my fear had really been. I couldn't lose someone else. I had prayed that I could move past the argument this morning and now it all felt so small.

He brushed his hand through my hair and held me back, his hand moving from my hair to my face. It was still pouring and cars passed by on the highway. I was freezing, drenched with rain, and none of it mattered at all. His fingertips outlined my face, from my hair, down my jawline, and to my chin. He stood close to me and I noticed I was holding my breath. Looking down at me, he drew me closer and went to say something…

"Luca!!! You're ok!!" Kate plowed into Luca's waist, again causing him to slightly grimace as her little body hit his mending wound. But still, he lifted her eagerly into a bear hug as the others joined us. "I knew you would be," she said confidently.

Linc came beside us with Sam who I caught a side eye and smirk from, as she leaned into hug Luca too. I stepped back, a little uneasy and embarrassed, shaking off the trance I had been in.

After our reunion, we took cover back in the woods. The rain began to calm down, and we started walking the two miles up the tree line to another exit, where Luca left the car. He knew taking out cash from the ATM would surely draw attention, although I thought that odd. *Were the Guard really watching our bank accounts?* But I didn't say anything. The details didn't really matter with us all together and safe.

Linc and Luca had decided, the night before, that Luca should look over the cars before ever taking the money out. If he knew going in, which one it would be, he'd need to make the transaction in cash as quickly as possible. Luca had to pay Donnie, the dealer, an extra thousand to give us a registered car. The payment acted as assurance that he wouldn't disclose his name or the car's registration to the Guard, should they show up. After forty-five hundred dollars, a three-mile run, being chased by the guard, and a happy reunion, we were the proud owners of a rusted, silver Pontiac Grand Prix, made before any of us were even born.

Chapter 10

THAT NIGHT, AFTER A THREE-HOUR DRIVE NORTH, WE FOUND A motel at the base of the mountains called The CreekBeds, which looked sketchier than the car dealership. Its logo had the outline of a man yelling *vacancy* in bright-red, glowing letters. I imagined they were always vacant. It was desolate. The rooms were cheap and outdated, and hardly maintained. But we finally felt safe, and hopefully, closer to Caleb. We stayed in one room, with the cash Luca retrieved from the ATM and I felt secure knowing we were all together. We each took turns to shower, hanging wet clothes on the motel heater and over the bathroom door to dry. I was so thankful we each had a set of spare clothes.

When my turn for the bathroom came, I couldn't believe what I looked like after only one day of travel. My hair, dirty-blonde and wavy, was matted and knotted throughout my head. My face and hands were filthy and I was sure my converse would never be the same. I took them to the shower with me, rinsing them on the tub floor as I rinsed the grime from my body. Red clay leaked from the soles, staining the base of the tub and leaving a ring of caked dirt on its walls.

I felt guilty about how long I stood there, letting the hot water run over my head and down my back. I was cold to the bone after being in wet clothes for the entirety of the day and the shower's heat brought back life to my finger tips and toes. My body showed the effects of small snacks and few meals, mixed with long distance walking and running over the past few weeks. I was thinner than I probably ever had been.

My mind raced at everything that passed that day, but mostly a feeling of relief at the day's success and Luca's safety resonated within me. My stomach growled, ravenous after all that we had been through without food. I decided rest would help the hunger dissipate, so I reluctantly cleaned the shower behind me, dried off, and dressed in the gray v-neck and black sweatpants I had set aside.

Pulling up my hair into a fast bun, I smelled distinctively… burgers. I swung the door open hard and was almost brought to tears by the sight of the feast before me. The guys decided to get us all a real meal from a diner down the street. Their giant smiles as I entered the room beamed with happiness at the treasure they had produced for us all. After they each showered and everyone was settled, we feasted on burgers, fries, milkshakes, and Coca-Cola. We fell asleep full that night. Sam and Linc, cradled together on a queen bed, Kate and I on the other, and Luca on the floor between us all.

When we all slept until ten a.m. the next day, we decided it would be best to use funds to stay another night. We were sore, tired, and had no plan for where to go from there. Getting on the road would prove useless if we didn't know which direction we were going in. The motel was about three hours north of our hometown. Far enough to not run into anyone we may know, but still not without the presence of the Guard. I wasn't sorry to stay in the dinky motel room. Our quarters were tight, but the day allowed us to wash clothes in a washing machine at the motel, a luxury we hadn't enjoyed in weeks.

In the afternoon, we shared a peanut butter cracker lunch before Sam, Linc, and Kate went to wash our laundry, leaving Luca and I alone in the room. I wondered if they us that way on purpose. Sam was particularly good at orchestrating things that way, but I acted like it didn't send my stomach into my throat as soon as the door shut behind them. I sat on the floor in the corner of the room, wrapped in a geometric-printed comforter I pulled off of one of the beds, and opened the text to the second book of Timothy. Scanning the worn pages I looked for anything highlighted, something to draw my attention from my heart beating as fast as it was.

Verse five,

> *I am reminded of your sincere faith, a faith*
> *That dwelt first in your grandmother.......*

I glanced up. And back down again when I saw that he, too, was distractedly reading. Taking a breath, I refocused.

> *and your mother....and now, I am sure,*
> *dwells in you as well.*

I felt a sense of shame reading those words. Did I have the faith of my grandparents, of my parents—or of Caleb? I wasn't so sure. I had pushed the pain of losing my family as deep down as I possibly could. It had been weeks and I focused most of my attention on not thinking of them. On not mourning their losses. When I thought of them: of Mama fluttering through the kitchen, of Daddy's last glance at me in the woods, of Caleb holding my hand on the way home, the hurt threatened to overcome me. I couldn't allow myself to fall apart. I couldn't allow myself to think about my parents. *Why them and not me? What was happening to Caleb now? Was he even alive?* I had to believe he was.

What's more is that I hated the people who had done this to us. Christ said to pray for them, and I hoped the worst for them. I hoped they'd pay for what they had done to my family and to so many others. A righteous anger and fear of the unknown filled me to the brim. I knew… my faith was weaker than I could have ever previously imagined.

Embarrassed, I felt like my inner most thoughts could certainly be heard across the tiny room.

I glanced up again, and this time, my eyes met Luca's as he asked, "What are you reading, Vala?"

"2nd Timothy," I answered apprehensively.

He smiled slightly, "Would you read some to me?"

I nodded and shakily started where I left off,

> *For this reason I remind you to fan*
> *into flame the gift of God, which is in you*
> *through the laying on of hands,*
> *for God gave us a spirit not of fear,*
> *but of power and love and self-control.*

"And what do you think of that?" He asked when I paused at the end of the seventh verse . His genuineness set me at ease answering.

"I guess I think—I feel like—I feel like I always have a spirit of fear. Especially now, after all that's happened. And I obviously don't have much self-control or Christ-filled love for others. I mean, look at how I treated everyone yesterday. I was so quick to anger and fear. I was terrified we'd be caught. That, you'd be caught…"

He was quiet for a minute after my admission and Luca graciously disagreed saying, "I don't think that's true at all. I think you've been incredibly brave after all that you've been through. None of us could have imagined what we would find when we went to your house that day, Vala. What you went through...."

He thought for a minute before continuing and a lump rose into my throat, "Think about the night you came to warn us at the Hall's house, you were the one who got the car, you stitched me up." His tone changed a bit. He was more gentle somehow, "and yesterday, that was just a misunderstanding. We should have been upfront with you about my car and about the plans Linc and I made. But you, running as far as you did..." the last bit trailed off.

Had he gotten embarrassed thinking of the rest stop? I felt my own cheeks warm thinking of it. I didn't know what to say. We sat there for a minute, and it wasn't awkward at all. It was just quiet between us. Comfortable. He opened up his Bible and began to read where I left off. I curled further into the comforter, content to hear him read this time.

The verses spoke of suffering for the Gospel's sake, knowing that God's purpose and grace would be made known. I liked the way his voice said the words so confidently. He was bold and sure. We started to talk more openly, making me feel more confident as well. It was easy, really, talking like this to him. Almost like talking to Sam, or even to Caleb.

The others came back and before long we all were sitting across the two queen beds, discussing strategies for the coming days, while sharing potato chips and candy bars gathered from the laundry room's vending machine. Kate, laying on her belly across the floor where Luca had slept, drew pictures reminiscent of the wildflowers we had seen the day before. She inhaled M&M's absentmindedly as we talked around her. The four of us kept conversation light, knowing her ears were not out of reach. Our information on Guard camps was little, at best.

"I've... heard youth are taken North to camps," Luca said, but with a hint of uncertainty and grief.

"I mean, that's helpful, right?" I said, trying to encourage him and myself. Any information was better than none at all.

Sam agreed, "Yeah, its somethin' to go on. You're right, Vala."

Linc looked at Luca and then to Sam and I, who were sitting opposite of them on the bed. "It is helpful, but we don't know where the camp is or if Caleb was even brought to that one."

"Or how to get him out," Luca added.

From the floor, Kate popped up from her drawing, "Couldn't we just stay here? I love the cheeseburgers at the diner."

Hers was a welcome interruption, as it usually was. "Ya know what Katie, that's a pretty good idea," Linc answered her and I knew he was serious about it.

I felt disheartened, but not without hope.

I wanted desperately to do something useful to find Caleb, but we were limited. Youth were taken to camps, but not always killed. I chose to hold on to that. If we were to gather any more information ultimately we needed money, permanent shelter, and somewhere safe to hide in plain sight. After Kate's suggestion and lots of discussion, we decided, it couldn't be done without jobs. So for the time being, we'd call the motel home.

Chapter 11

Jobs came easily in that part of town. Lincoln and Luca found jobs with a construction crew, cleaning up highways and side streets. They didn't have to have IDs for the work and it paid well. Working construction sites during summer, in the south, couldn't have been easy, but they never complained. Luca grew tanner and Linc's already mocha skin grew darker and darker during those summer months working. And both were noticeably stronger, going to work some days before the sun came up and then coming home after a full day, exhausted from manual labor. Linc's body transformed seemingly overnight, from a tall and relatively gangly teen to a muscular man. Luca's body too, although already much more defined and muscular than Linc's to begin with, had changed. His brown hair had lightened in the summer sun, which made his eyes seem greener than I thought possible. His chest and shoulders had broadened even more with the arduous work. I attempted, poorly, to not take notice often.

We decided to pay weekly to stay at the same motel where rooms were cheap and Sam was able to get a job cleaning rooms. Kate tagged along with her beginning in the early morning hours, from room to room helping occasionally, and completing homework that we each created for her at night: math, English, and writing. Kate also grew noticeably over the summer. We had to replace her shoes twice within a month, along with secondhand shopping for new clothes to keep up with her growth spurts. Sam as she always had, mothered her and took care to make sure Kate kept up with school, was well nourished, and generally content.

Sam really took to mothering us all, in her own ways. She ensured that Lincoln and Luca were sent to work each day with a lunch and water bottles. She checked in with me daily with a, "How are you doing, Vala? How are you, really?" She sometimes asked, although tentatively, about my nightmares.

To which I normally replied with, "They're actually going away," or, "they aren't so bad anymore." She never pushed, but I knew she didn't believe me. I adored her genuine love for us all, and her intuitive ability to know exactly when I needed someone to talk to. On the weekends, she and I would sneak away to do laundry, where we could talk in private about the guys, about life, and about our dreams for the future. It was almost as it had been before.

I found work at the diner close to the motel, *Papa's Place*. The owner, a kind family man everyone called Papa, gave me a waitressing job with no questions asked. His wife had passed away years before, so he had raised his daughter alone while also keeping the diner afloat. It stayed relatively busy, with truckers and vacationers coming through regularly, especially during the summer and fall months. And thankfully, members of the Guard were rarely spotted there. It seemed he needed the help and I was available at just the right time.

I worked the morning shift to late afternoon, and sometimes through the dinner rush if Papa needed me. I began my shift before the others woke up, opening the diner early to make sure everything was ready for the day's first customers. I savored my early morning walk to Papa's, the morning sky still dark and wispy with purple clouds, making way for the sun. I used the time to pray or to sing Mama's old worship songs to myself.

The front of the diner had a large window reaching from one end to the other. It faced East, and provided a brilliant sunrise each morning, shining golden light across the black and white tiled floors and clean white countertops and tables. Breakfast was usually a busy rush of customers, some just wanting a quick cup of coffee while others sat until early afternoon, refilling their cups and their bellies.

Papa had been kind to my makeshift family, always giving a little something extra on their plates or even letting Luca and Lincoln come in early before opening for a quick breakfast before work. The first morning that Linc decided not to come, Luca asked if he could walk me to work. I didn't mind the company and Luca didn't make me as nervous as he once did, so I agreed.

He set our pace, slow, enjoying the fresh morning air, "There's something about being out here that is really freeing. Don't you think?" He took a deeper breath than normal, " I love the mountains and the warm air first thing in the morning."

I felt the same. I felt free. It was a relief to live life, outside of the fear of the Guard, but it also brought along with it resounding guilt.

I answered simply, "Yeah. I do."

He looked away from me, sensing my discomfort. "We haven't forgotten him, Vala. We won't forget him." His pace stayed the same, but he turned back to me once more, "You think about him a lot, don't you? About Caleb?"

I nodded. Afraid if I spoke, a floodgate of emotion would follow. "We'll find him," he put his arm around me, pulling me a little closer to himself, "I promise we'll find him."

After that morning, Luca came to the diner for breakfast alone at least once a week, always walking me there himself. Our talks on the way to work were much lighter than the first morning. Sometimes we'd talk about what life was like before all of this started. He had a love for basketball, which is how he came to befriend Lincoln, and for reading. He lit up when he summarized his favorite books, most of which were classic adventures like *The Swiss Family Robinson* or *The Hatchet*. I talked mainly about my friendship with Sam. How we spent evenings afterschool dancing in her living room or weekends at the movie theater with friends.

Sometimes we talked about the future and what we thought we'd do with our lives, before any of this had happened. "I always thought I'd be an artist," I admitted one morning, when he asked me simply, "What do you want to be, Vala?"

He seemed genuinely shocked at my admission, "But, I've never seen any of your work?" I immediately wished I had said something else like "I want to be a teacher," or, "a nurse," but knew him well enough now to know that he would not relent until I told him more.

"I've always just kept them for myself, I guess. My drawings, that is. Or I guess they're more like sketches."

He kept pace beside me, "And you've never shown them to anyone?"

I hesitated, "I really only showed Sam sometimes and my Dad. He loves—He loved art." I fumbled with my apron ties, absent-mindedly, "What about you? What do you want to do?"

"Hmmm, that's tough," he considered for a minute before answering, "I honestly don't know. Not now, anyways." It was a minimal confession, I thought, but not an invulnerable one. What could any of us do, or plan to do now?

At the diner, Luca usually sat quietly reading and drinking a cup of coffee or water. I loved having him there, and Linc whenever he joined. It felt like a piece of home carried along with me into a strange place. It was a comfort to set up the tables or to prep coffee with Luca nearby. Those became my favorite mornings, although I wouldn't admit it to anyone else, least of all to him.

Papa's daughter, Sarah, worked the afternoon and evening shift. She was a year younger than I was, saving money for college. She wanted to go to school to become a nurse, like her Mother had been. Sarah was light-hearted and kind, much like her dad. I never saw her without a small braid on the side of her head, which pulled back her short blond hair. She'd make customers laugh as she served them, always charming and vivacious. We had a fast friendship working side by side each day of the summer. Sarah's extroverted spirit was magnetic to my more reserved nature. Her energy was infectious and I looked forward to afternoons when I knew she'd be there, making me laugh along with all of her customers. Papa adored her, always making sure he asked about her day before setting her to work. And like Papa, she welcomed me and the others into their lives graciously.

However, I never seemed to notice just how charismatic or how pretty Sarah really was until the end of my shift, on nights when Luca, Linc, Sam, and Kate would come to the diner for dinner. She'd serve them as any other customers, usually while I did clean-up and other chores before clocking out. They'd join in on her antics, laughing, telling jokes, and sometimes filling the whole diner with the sound of their voices talking over each other.

She seemed to pay extra attention to Luca, who even after working hard jobs day in and day out, had no problem making casual conversation with her easily. They made each other laugh and it made me uncomfortable in a way that I never wanted anyone to know. I took note on how she studied him, when she wasn't at their table. And I had seen him, on at least one occasion, embrace her as he had me on our first morning walk. They looked good beside each other. His strong, tan frame accentuated her soft, sweet femininity.

It made my heart ache to see them together, but I pushed it

away. Why should it? I loved Sarah. She had become a dear friend to me and to all of my friends. And Luca didn't belong to me. Far from it. Of course we talked more and more, but nothing had happened like the night at the rest stop, and neither of us brought it up. It was a momentary fluster that disappeared as quickly as it happened. I assumed he was embarrassed or thought little of it. Regardless, he had become one of my closest friends. And seeing his interactions with a beautiful, carefree girl like Sarah illuminated a longing inside of me that started to feel hard to deny.

Days and weeks turned to months. We started a life in that small town, just outside of the mountains, and The CreekBeds motel became our home. We visited the local farmer's market in town when we felt it was safe to do so. Treating ourselves to fresh peaches and boiled peanuts after walking in and out of the market's stalls for a morning. And spent time exploring the woods and creek behind our motel on weekends when we weren't working. We worshipped from the safety of our motel room and continued our routine of praying together daily.

Kate turned eleven at the end of May, and then Luca's nineteenth birthday followed in June. We celebrated both with burgers and pies from the diner, with Sarah joining us after her shift. On both occasions she insisted that the occupants of the diner sing as loudly as possible. Kate embraced the attention, standing on the booth bench and directing the birthday song with her fingers waving back and forth as an orchestra conductor would. Sarah called for encores and applause beside her, cheering her on and making her giggle with glee. Luca shrunk distinctively into his seat, when his turn came, clearly uncomfortable with the attention of the diner solely on him. Although, he did hug and thank Sarah later that night for making his birthday a special one.

Sarah never asked questions about what we were all doing in town together, content to just befriend us without obligation. I was thankful she didn't need details. I wondered if her father had told her not to ask. Dad had assured me, years before, that Remnant sympathizers would show up in times of need. I thought as time passed that maybe Papa was one of them. Maybe, eventually, we'd be able to trust him with our secret.

When Sam's eighteenth birthday came around in August, we spent our Saturday off at the creek behind the motel. Luca got up early to get us all coffee, and orange juice for Kate, to take along. We packed a picnic lunch, played and wrestled in the water, and napped in the sun all day. We even found a rope swing after walking along the creek and used it to swing across and drop into a larger ravine. Each of us screamed with delight when it was our turn to cross.

My cheeks were sun kissed by the afternoon and my heart was full. I laid back content, with arms outstretched behind my head on the warm soil beneath me, soaking in the heat of the day. I breathed in the sounds of the water passing me by and the gentle breeze moving the leaves throughout the tree tops. Like a moving painting before me, the colors and textures of that day flooded into my very spirit. These would be our last few days of summer, before cooler air rushed in and the colors changed in the mountains.

I watched as Kate splashed Luca by surprise. He grabbed her up with ease and swung her by the arms, with the tips of her toes just touching the face of the water as she laughed uncontrollably. Luca's joy, playing in the water with Kate, was unmatched. He beamed at her as an older brother would a younger sister. Her squeals of happiness filled the otherwise quiet woods. Sam floated on top of the tiny, creek bed rapids, resting her head with her eyes closed on Linc's chest behind her. It was easy to rest there, at the base of the mountains. We were free.

I assumed we'd celebrate Sam's birthday in the evening with pies at Papa's Place, as we had the others. Instead, Lincoln gave her a ring by the side of the creek that day. It was a simple, gold band with a knot forming at the top and it fit her perfectly. I wasn't surprised that they wanted to get married this young. They had been together for years and friends since we were toddlers. There were no dates set, or dresses bought, just excitement and pure joy from us all. It felt right to make plans for our future, even if it was pretty hazy.

Papa treated everyone to milkshakes that evening, with he and Sarah joining in on the party. Sam spent the entire night teary-eyed and glowing with happiness, and Lincoln stayed by her side as he always did. As he always would. We celebrated in the diner hours past closing, talking and laughing and teasing. Almost forgetting about the circumstances that brought us all together in the first place.

By September we had saved quite a bit of money. The summer had been rich with tips, construction jobs, and steady income, along with the sense of peace and safety we found there. God provided in abundance. We were able to pay for food and motel expenses, and set aside anything that may be used for the future. We settled into a rhythm there. And even started renting a separate room for Linc and Luca, which was better for space, the shared bathroom, and created some separation for Linc and Sam until they could be married.

After all of our months there though, we still had very little information on where the Guard camps may be. Fear kept us from approaching anyone in town to ask questions. We hadn't met open believers and we couldn't take a risk trusting strangers. It was odd enough for a group of teenagers to be lingering around at the motel and diner in this small mountain town. Asking the wrong people could surely lead to more trouble. I felt guilty, much of the time, for living a life disconnected from the pain I was sure Caleb was enduring. I knew I could do little to change our circumstances, but my own lack of action tormented me internally.

The truth was, I felt content. I was generally happy. And I hated that I was capable of happiness after the darkness that stole my family. While contentment reigned over my days, my nights were not as undisturbed. My dreams of Mama and Daddy, telling me to find Caleb and to search for Micah, took over as time passed and it was rare that I had a full night's sleep. I knew Sam and Kate had grown used to them too, as they stopped asking me if I was okay when I'd wake up screaming or drenched in tears. I wondered if they told Linc and Luca about my troubles sleeping, but I never asked.

 Our contentment and safety led to inactivity in our search. The bitter truth was, we were no closer to finding Caleb or Micah then we were the night they found me in the woods. It didn't seem we'd ever get to either of them.

Chapter 12

On a Tuesday morning in late September, I worked a normal shift at the diner. I always arrived early to beat the breakfast crowd, so getting in by five thirty wasn't out of the ordinary. As I walked up though, I noticed the familiar, ominous black SUVs sitting, waiting in the parking lot. My heart dropped into my gut. I had already walked too far into sight of the diner and the bay window that extended across the front of the building that I knew it'd be too suspicious to turn around. Inwardly, I began to panic. *Were they there for me? For us?* Sarah, met me unusually in the parking lot on her way to school, stopping me before I could step through the door.

She looked nervous, but determined, "Vala! Give me a hug." This was an unusual greeting from her. We had never hugged before, but I walked into her embrace awkwardly, only to have her cling tight to me with a whisper in my ear. She spoke as fast as I had ever heard her, "Dad sent me out to school early to warn you.

You're his niece. Here from the West Coast to work in the diner. Now smile and wave as I leave. Got it?"

A gasp caught in my throat and I held back tears as she began to pull away. He knew. Papa knew all of this time and never said anything to us. I did as she said.

Heart pounding and hands shaking, I released her and said shakily, "See ya later, Sarah," barely getting the words out. Taking a deep breath and praying for steadiness, I walked in and acted as normally as possible.

"Good Morning, Papa," I mustered, surprising even myself. Should I call him Papa? I mean, wasn't he supposed to be my uncle? I didn't recognize the two members of the Guard, dressed in dark suits as they always were. They both wore severe expressions and one looked like he was my age.

What if they had come specifically for us? Had we been too careless here? It had been foolish to live so openly in this town. Had they already found the others? What would happen to us? That familiar terror rooted into my spirit within as I tried to remain calm and unaffected for the men, who I was sure were studying me. Then, a small voice whispered within me, *God did not give you a spirit of fear...*

Papa seemed completely unaffected by the visitors at the counter, "Mornin', Vala. Please get straight to settin' up. I'm almost done with these gentlemen." He gestured for me to go to the back. His southern drawl ever courteous and carefree. "My niece, Vala, has been workin' for me ever since my sister died last year. She came from out west. She may go off to school next year, but we'll see."

The older man stiffened and I felt him look in my direction, "That's an unusual name, Vala. Where'd it come from?"

My name sounded foreign on the strangers lips and I hesitated with how to answer, when the younger of the two men interrupted and asked suspiciously, "Your niece calls you *Papa*?"

"Ha. Yeah, everyone calls me that. Started as a teenager. Even my own Mama called me that once it caught on. I used to take care of my younger siblins' and...."

"Yeah okay, we get it," the older man interrupted him this time and forgetting his original question, warned him, "like we were telling you before, we're watching you Mr. Joyner. Sympathizers are penalized to the full extent of the law. If you are aiding criminals, we *will* find out."

"I assure you, gentlemen, I understand," Papa answered them graciously, "you sure I can't get you both some coffee to go?" He was walking them towards the door, but they never answered. I heard the bell hanging over the entry ring as they left.

I waited there in the kitchen, making myself busy with prep work, and wondering what I would say to Papa when he came to confront me. But he never did.

Instead, I heard him up front greeting a couple who walked in, and then eventually calling for me, "Vala, we have hungry customers. Let's get to work."

I worked all day, never having time to sit down, and yet, it felt like the longest day of work thus far. My hands shook as I refilled cups of coffee and soda and scribbled breakfast and lunch orders across a tattered notebook. I stumbled and stammered throughout the day, I'm sure raising the suspicions of at least a few customers.

An older lady, eating a grilled-ham sandwich alone in a booth at the far end of the diner, even asked me at one point, "Are you ok, honey? You need to sit down?" I was incapable of acting like the morning hadn't happened and completely unhinged not knowing if the others were safe. Should I even stay?

I avoided Papa's eyes and conversation. My mind raced endlessly throughout the day. *Would he get scared of the Guard and turn us in? How would I warn the others not to come in that night for dinner, if they were even safe? Where would we go now?* I tried pushing the fear away and prayed the Guard would not come again. I knew, though, that eventually they would. And Papa risked his life, and Sarah's, if he didn't turn us over.

My shift ended just before the dinner rush. Papa called me over to the register, out of ear shot from a few customers finishing up their afternoon coffee and slices of pie. I walked to him reluctantly, unsure of how I should respond.

Without pausing from his work at the register he began speaking quietly, "The others were warned earlier, after our visitors left this mornin'. Your shift is over now, understand me? You're gonna go to the back exit, off the kitchen, and wait there for Luca to pick ya up. And then wait at your room until I can get there tonight. This is important— do not leave the Creekbed."

He turned towards me, gently putting his hands on my shoulders and forcing me to look at him, "You can trust me. Okay, Vala? I'll be there tonight." And I believed him. Astonished at his directness, and grateful for his discretion, I nodded, said goodbye as casually as I could, and went straight to the back exit as he had instructed me.

Luca was already waiting for me in the back. He startled me, jumping up quickly from leaning against the back door, and pulling me into a tight squeeze as soon as he saw me. Relief flooded his face.

He whispered tenderly into my ear, "Are you okay?" I nodded, my head wedged underneath his chin, comforted by his arms. He continued, holding me close as he spoke, "I'm sorry I couldn't come sooner." His fingers combed through my hair and I could feel his heart beating rapidly as he held me close to his chest. "Papa said to go about the day as normally as we could. I tried to convince Linc we should sneak away, but he thought it'd raise too many questions. We just had to pray and to trust."

I wondered aloud, pulling away from his arms to look at him, "Are Sam and Kate ok?" How did Papa tell you? He was at the diner with me all day." I was relieved to see him too and his familiar embrace had been the comfort I needed after the tension of the day. So much so that I realized I was holding the sides of his shirt tightly in my hands. I released a bit, hoping he hadn't noticed.

He smirked at the change in my hands and answered, "The girls are fine. Sam worked her shift like normal, with Kate following along. They've been waiting in your room ever since. Linc is with them now."

They were safe. I released the breath I felt I had been holding onto all day and Luca continued, "Sarah actually came to the construction site to warn us! I didn't even know she knew where we were working…." He trailed off and then lifted my chin with his hand, "Vala, I wanted to come right away, but Sarah said we shouldn't. She said Papa has a plan — I don't know what it is, but I—I'm so thankful you're safe." Pausing and looking at me for a second, he smiled again, "Let's go home, ok?" He gestured to the door and led me through, heading in the direction of the tree line behind the diner. We walked along it, instead of the road like we normally did in the mornings, toward the motel.

"So, did Sarah say anything else— about Papa's plan, that is?" I asked curiously.

He seemed as serious as before, but I noticed another quick smirk peek from the side of his mouth again as he answered, "Not much. She warned us about the Guard, obviously. She told us to stay put and that I should meet you at the end of your shift through the kitchen entrance of the diner. And that she'd see me later, with Papa at the motel."

"Just you? Wasn't Linc with you?"

"Um, yeah. Linc was there too," he answered, confused at the question.

"You said, she'd see *you* later. It was just weird how you said it, I guess."

It wasn't weird. Not in the slightest. We had no idea what laid ahead of us after the morning's events. Our lives could be at stake for all we knew, and yet, I could only seem to think about Sarah seeing Luca later. My tone said it all. And I knew my face did too. I tried to look away feigning disinterest so he wouldn't notice.

"Why are you so interested in what Sarah said, Vala? She really helped us today." He answered back, almost accusingly.

"Oh, I don't know. And, of course, I know she helped us. She and Papa both did." I rubbed my hands through my hair to keep busy. Exhaustion and stress clearly weakened the façade of indifference I usually tried to display towards Luca.

"I didn't mean anything by it. Let's just get home," I quipped, wanting to wiggle out of the situation I had put myself in. I skipped a step in an effort to walk ahead of him.

He grabbed my hand before I could put any real distance between us. "No. I think you did mean something. We're talking about this now," he argued, pulling me into the woods and past the path we were following. We were completely out of sight of the highway.

"What are you doing, Luca? This is not a big deal right now." I couldn't see how we had the time to stop there. He stood over me, staring into my face. Too close for comfort. Was he mad? His green eyes looked stern, but still gentle.

"Have I given you reason to think that I am interested in Sarah at all?"

Humiliated, I avoided his eyes. "Ummm. No, not really, but it would be okay... obviously. I wasn't implying...I mean. It *is* complicated, but she seems to really like you... and... I mean, she's so pretty, and sweet....I think you wou....I love Sarah. She's my friend. And you're my friend..." I fumbled through any coherent thoughts and he saw right through it.

"I think you would be great together." I managed to get a full sentence out with eye contact, but very little fervor.

"Why can't you just say what you *really* think, Vala? Haven't we been through enough together for you to be honest?!" It was an accusation. Infuriating. And embarrassing. And mostly true. "Why do you care so much about me and Sarah?"

I paced away from him for a minute in the woods, knowing his eyes followed me. I wished he'd say what was on *his* mind, but it was clear that I had brought this on myself. And I quite honestly, couldn't keep it in anymore.

"....Fine," I said, defeated, "do you think I'm proud? I don't want to feel this way." My voice was louder and shakier than I intended it to be. "You've become one of my best friends."

I hesitated, and then stood directly in front of him, forcing myself to address him fully, but keeping a safe distance between us, "I want you to be happy. I do." I meant it. "I really do."

He didn't flinch or take his eyes off of mine, so I went on, "But I hate the way I feel when I see you laugh or talk or even look at Sarah. It's not just that she's beautiful and kind and lovable. I know I'd feel this way about any girl, anywhere—with you."

Why wasn't he saying anything?

I felt the words spilling out of me, a floodgate opened, "And I know we never talked about the night at the rest stop. And that's fine. But I felt like..."

He moved closer to me now.

I stumbled over my thoughts at his movement, "I thought you were...since that night you....after all this time..."

He stood close enough to touch me.

Defeated and humiliated I blurted out, "I wish it was me." I could feel the tears welling up.

But then he was cupping my face with his hands and drawing it towards his.

"Vala, It *is* you. It's only you."

He was sincere. His hair fell into his face as he spoke. And then his lips connected with mine and I forgot everything around us, the trees, the diner, the cars in the distance…Sarah. He stepped back for a minute and we both laughed. The tension between us finally released.

"I've wanted to do that since the gym." It was an honest confession, but Luca didn't seem embarrassed at all to make it.

"Really?" I felt so silly. He thought of *me*? In the gym. "I mean, I *am* an excellent doctor." He laughed with his face close to mine and grabbed me up again. And I was safe and warm and content and chosen.

Chapter 13

THE MOTEL ROOM WAS MUCH MORE TENSE THAN OUR SPOT IN the woods. Linc, Sam, and Kate had been waiting for us, anxiously. I felt guilty, knowing that we wasted precious time with our friends worrying about us, but I couldn't be sorry for what had happened between Luca and I. I felt so much more secure knowing that he was really by my side.

We had stayed in the woods only a short time. He wrapped me in his arms for much of it, talking through the months following the night at the rest stop. How he convinced Linc to give him one morning a week alone with me at the diner and had prayed for the right time to tell me how he felt. When we talked on that first walk about Caleb, he decided to wait a little longer, not wanting to put extra pressure on me.

And Luca kissed me. I melted into his affections. The tension had been building for all of those months before. But his desire for my heart, his longing to serve me, to walk beside me, to know me well, to sit in the diner alone to be with me— those things endeared him to me all the more. The moments we shared in the woods together would replay in my head, I was sure, for the rest of my life. And although we didn't mention anything about the woods to the others, like a mother, Sam read my thoughts as we walked through the door of the motel room.

"Where have you guys been? It shouldn't have taken you that long. Did you run into trouble on the way?" Lincoln bombarded us with questions and a scolding tone as soon as we closed the door to the room the girls and I had been sleeping in.

"No trouble at all. We just took our time, Linc. I didn't want to look suspicious," Luca answered smoothly, trying to set him at ease.

Sam, though, looked between us, smirking at me and then Luca. It was uncharacteristic, especially considering the circumstances. She knew. I knew it. I couldn't hide anything from her.

Sam grabbed Lincoln's hand with understanding and said, "Babe, why don't you give us some time to get settled. Vala looks exhausted," Everyone turned to look at me again as she continued with what I knew was somehow a mixture of genuine and simulated concern, "Let's give her some space to get cleaned up and refreshed a bit. I'm sure she's had an emotional day. It's been hard on all of us."

She looked towards me for a second as she spoke, so I yawned to the side and nodded, playing into her motherly ploy for time alone. "You guys go back to your room and just let us know when Papa and Sarah show up, ok? I'll fill Vala in on everything we've decided," she instructed as she basically pushed them out of our room. Linc left hesitantly, but without further arguments with Sam. Luca winked at me slyly as they left, a grin growing at the corners of his mouth. I thought I may explode of embarrassment, knowing Sam most definitely saw him.

When the door closed behind them, Sam turned with a giant grin on her face,

"VALA!" She was already giggling and hugging me with relief from the day's events.

"What?" I tried to play it cool, soaking in her hug.

"What happened out there? Luca went to get you over an hour ago! We were so worried about you all day," she paused and then grinned from ear to ear mischievously, "it looks like we were right to send Luca though." She nudged me playfully with her elbow. I looked at Kate watching us talk back and forth.

Sam caught on right away. "Katie girl, will you do some writing homework for me? Vala and I need to chat about the crazy day."

"Ugh, yes," Kate got down from her spot on the bed begrudgingly, to find a spot on the other side of the room, "but I already know that Luca has a crush on Vala."

Shocking us both, Sam and I laughed hysterically. We waited for Kate to get settled at the small table in our room before I divulged everything that happened from the morning and on.

"Oh Vala. I'm so glad this *finally* happened." She was breathless with excitement.

"I can't believe you are talking about this after the Guard being here today, and Papa knowing. There are way more important things goin' on, Sam." I added in, "And, besides, I really didn't think he was interested. So I don't know what you mean by *finally*." It actually made me feel incredible self-conscious. Was everyone more aware than I was?

She looked at me, almost annoyed. "Obviously today was serious. But, we have to live, Vala. I want to live. I want to be excited for you, even if it's in the middle of— whatever it was that happened today." She rested her hand in mine, "It's so easy to see that Luca adores you. For months I've been praying this would happen. Did he talk to you about anything else?"

She seemed hesitant. It was an odd question and I didn't know what she could mean, but I thought nothing of it. "No. He told me how he felt about me. How he had been interested, even before all of this happened to us. He noticed me when he moved here. Can you believe that? He's been praying about whether he should talk to me about it." I could hear the astonishment in my own voice.

Sam leaned in from the spot she sat on across from me, dropping her voice to a whisper, "And did he kiss you?"

I gave a coy smile and ignored the question completely. Of course, driving Sam crazy. She didn't need all of the finer details. As much as I loved her, like a sister, I wanted to keep some of the afternoon with Luca to myself. I really was exhausted, and I was anxious to know what we were going to talk to Papa about. And how much we should tell him about ourselves.

Changing the subject I asked, "What did you decide about Papa? You said you guys decided something before the guys left."

Sam wasn't fooled, but she relented, "Yes, okay. The guys and I talked after they got home today. Obviously we were terrified. We basically had to keep Luca strapped to a chair until it was time to pick you up." She smiled at this and continued, "But, we think we *have* to trust Papa and Sarah. I mean, why wouldn't we? He could have turned you in today. Really they could have turned any of us in and they didn't. Sarah came to warn us all as soon as she left the diner this morning. That has to mean something."

I agreed, "I actually think he may have known all along."

She looked curious, "Really? Do you think so?"

"Yeah, I do. I don't know why. I just got the feeling today. It's like he already had a plan in case the Guard showed up."

She seemed at peace, which set me at ease as well, "I think he's going to help us, Vala. Maybe...," she hesitated, "maybe somehow he'll lead us to Caleb."

I hoped that by some miracle that would be true. Regardless of what Papa had to say that night, however, the group decided that we couldn't stay here any longer. Not after the Guard had come so close. Although we didn't know where we'd go from here, it was time to move on.

I decided that I really did need to clean up after the crazy day. I was able to take a moment to breathe and just clear my head, as

I stood in the hot steam, allowing the water to fall down my back. So much had happened in the course of twelve hours, and now what was to come? All was quiet and at peace, even in the midst of such uncertainty, and I knew I could have passed easily into sleep if given the opportunity.

Convincing myself to join the others, I got out. Allowing my wavy wet hair, which hadn't been cut in months, to hang far past my shoulders to dry. The fall brought with it crisp air in the mornings and evenings, and that night was no different. I chose my favorite pair of sweatpants to wear and a long-sleeved, gray t-shirt before leaving the sanctuary of the bathroom.

A small panic set in though, when I opened the bathroom door to find an abandoned room. Sam and Kate were gone. I quickly found a note, scribbled on the motel's stationary, laying on the floor at the front door. Sam directed me to come to the guys' room when I finished. Papa was already there.

The smell of burgers from the diner filled the air of their motel room. I assumed he brought us dinner, although it was clear no one had touched them. Linc, Sam, Kate, and Luca sat quietly on a bed together, the familiar faded, geometric bedspread beneath them. Papa and another man, who I didn't recognize, sat on the bed across from them. They looked like they were getting a scolding.

Everyone looked up when I came in, while Luca jumped up from his spot and motioned for me to sit next to him at the end of the bed. Everyone shuffled over so that I could join them.

Papa finally broke the silence, "Vala, I was just introducin' the others to my friend, John. You can trust him."

"He's one of the Remnant, Vala," Lincoln assured me, but he sounded guarded.

"How can we be sure we can trust either of you? And where's Sarah? She said she'd be here," I asked, ignoring the other man, and. directing my question to Papa. I was thankful Papa hadn't turned us in earlier, but I didn't know this man. Papa and Sarah had been kind to us for months, but John was a stranger. He was a risk.

"I could have turned ya'll in at any point over the past four months. Five kids, livin' out of a motel day to day. I'm simple, Vala, but I'm not stupid. It's a small town and we've had members pass through here and there. That's how I met John. He's here to help ya'll."

Papa paused to see if we had any response to that, but when none of us answered he continued, "Now, as far as Sarah's concerned, I wouldn't let her come. I trust ya'll and we care 'bout ya, but Remnant business is dangerous. Ya'll can see her at another time."

John, who had been observing us quietly up until that point, addressed me now. "Vala…" Realization passed across his face, "You aren't Vala Lee are you? You're Joel and Evie Lee's daughter?"

My heart stopped. Shocked, I nodded and felt Luca's body tense beside me.

I noticed Papa twitch at the sound of my last name, and I interjected, "I'm sorry I lied to you about my last name, Papa."

He replied simply, "I had my suspicions. It's alrigh' now."

I stuttered slightly, looking back to John, "How… how did you know?"

John answered with an air of excitement, "We knew your parents, Vala. Both Papa and I did. They were strong in faith. They helped found our settlement in the mountains. We hoped we'd find you eventually or that you'd come to us. Especially after what happened to your brother and to your parents."

I jumped off the bed at the mention of Caleb, "What happened to my brother?! Do you know where he is? Is he alive?"

John put his hand out towards me, just as Luca did the same from the back, pulling me closer to him rather than to this stranger, "I just meant when he was taken. Vala, we have intel that gives us reason to believe that Caleb is living in one of the camps not far from here." He looked to the others behind me, still sitting on the bed silently. "We could look into all of your families if you'd like."

Kate looked excitedly at Sam, who gave her a squeeze around her shoulders, and exchanged a glance with Lincoln knowingly. I could tell, she was not hopeful that news of their families would be positive. Luca slipped his hand into mine more firmly and pulled me down towards the bed to rejoin them. I hadn't realized how selfish my search for Caleb had been, all along ignoring the fact that Linc, the girls, and Luca all had families as well. And they knew little about their fates.

Despite that realization, I asked, "Do you know how we could get him out? Caleb I mean".

"I'm afraid it's impossible. No one has gone into a camp willingly and come out again," John sounded sincere, "at least not that I'm aware of."

"I have a question," Sam interrupted us, "what do you mean her parents founded your settlement?"

I started to process fully once Sam asked. *This stranger knew my parents. Caleb was alive. Papa knew my parents. He knew we were believers. My parents formed a settlement?* Luca put his fingers over mine on the bed and gave me a reassuring smile, as if he could see my internal thoughts and confusion playing out before him. I felt his thumb rubbing my hand tenderly.

John answered her, "There's a small settlement of believers, of the Remnant left in the mountains. We've used it as a safe haven for the past two years. Although, your parents helped planned the idea almost ten years ago, Vala."

He smiled at me with admiration in his voice at the mention of my parents again. "We have cabins, running water, a school for the kids," He smiled at Kate and she gushed at the acknowledgement as he continued, "I can take you all there. I'd just have to verify all of you through some questions to ensure we can trust you and keep our residents safe."

"Trust us?" Lincoln joined in the conversation. I was surprised it had taken him so long. "We don't even know if we want to go with you!"

"Linc, I think we shou…" Sam tried to speak, but he spoke over her objections.

"No, listen Papa, I'm grateful. I really am. That you didn't turn Vala in today, or any of us for that matter. You kept her safe today and we'll always be grateful for that. And I do trust *you*, but why would you just now be introducing us to John. If you've known all along who—what we were. Why not confront us sooner?"

Papa looked down at his hands, which were clamped together dangling from his knees. He was nodding his head. In agreement? But he said nothing.

It was John who responded, after a moment of quiet in the room, "Papa is under no obligation to connect believers together. He's a friend, who has kept your secret for months, at his own risk. He came to faith in Christ only in the past year and has chosen to remain in a dangerous position so that he may help when he's able, and when he feels led by the Lord. Until today, there was not an imminent threat to any of you."

John was methodical in how he spoke. He was clear and concise. His nature reminded me of my dad. He looked directly at Lincoln, "Although son, I'm afraid it was just a matter of time before you all were exposed. There are people in town who are not sympathetic to the Remnant followers, and who I suspect, we may have to thank for the visit from the Guard this morning."

He paused with a deep breath, and spoke with genuine concern, "You can't stay here, safely, anymore."

There was a finality in the way that John spoke, that no one dared argue with when he finished. I was left speechless, regardless. Papa was a believer. He protected me and our whole family and I'd never be able to thank him enough. My parents had this secret life I had no idea about. I may not know John, but Daddy and Mama did. And Papa did. And, I without a doubt, had trust in Papa.

"How long do we have to decide?" I asked, seriously considering going with this stranger.

"I can be back by Friday morning at dawn. But you'd have to be ready to go. We don't know how quickly the Guard will come back."

Lincoln went to speak, but I interrupted his efforts, "And if we go with you, will you help us find their families? And will you tell me which camp my brother is in?" I knew he didn't want to consent to my last demand, but John nodded.

Luca tensed beside me and interjected for the first time, "We need time to talk it over together. Alone." He looked at the four of us, rather than the two men sitting before us. John and Papa agreed, and we promised to have a decision, one way or another.

The others wanted to stay up and talk that night, but I didn't. Not in the slightest. The amount of information that I absorbed over the course of that day was too much to fully comprehend. From the stress of the morning, the woods with Luca, and now John, who had this secret connection to my parents. I felt overwhelmed with the weight of it all. How had they led a secret life outside of our family? How had I not seen it?

I tried to think back on meetings we weren't invited to and small trips my Mom and Dad took without Caleb and I, but they were few and far between. I thought back to the party we'd had at the house while my parents were away only two years before. They said they needed a getaway and we didn't ask any questions. I never told them about that party and neither had Caleb. It was our secret. Our little act of rebellion. And now I knew that they had been taking care of us more deeply than I could have imagined.

I snapped back to reality at the sound of my name, "Vala... Vala...are you even listening?" Linc looked irritated and stressed.

"Oh, I'm sorry. What did you say?" I shook out of the daydream and tried to sound interested.

Luca studied me with worry and leaned in close, "Are you okay? You're pretty distracted."

He didn't even wait for me to even respond when he looked at the others, "It's been a long day. Maybe we should table this for tomorrow."

"I'm fine. I'm just taking it all in, I guess. What were you all saying?"

Sam answered this time as Lincoln seemed more than exasperated with me, "We're deciding if it's worth the risk to go to the settlement with John. Or maybe we should move on from here further north."

I surprised myself with how sure I was and gave my answer without hesitation, "I'm going with John." I noticed Luca look down into his lap at my answer and Linc avoided my eyeline completely, "I don't expect that all of you will want to go, but he knows where Caleb is. I have to go with him."

In the midst of the uncomfortable silence and my acknowledgment of suddenly trusting a stranger, Kate joined my cause, "I want to go with John too. Please Sammy—Linc? I want to go to school. And maybe he knows where our Mama and Daddy are?"

Sam and Linc could deny her nothing and without saying a word, nodded in agreement with Kate and me. Everyone looked to Luca, who simply said, "I promised you we'd find Caleb. So we will."

It was settled. We'd be ready to go with John on Friday. I passed out on one of the beds quickly after our short debate, with Kate combing her fingers through my hair as I drifted off. The sound and familiarity of the others' voices talking softly nearby lulled me to sleep, and knowing they were in the room brought deep peace. We were together. We were safe, for now. And, at long last I knew, Caleb was alive.

I was running. Out of breath. Tears streamed down my face as I looked over my shoulder, over and over again, stumbling over low hanging branches and rocks. What was chasing me? What was I so afraid of? I didn't know. But I kept running. I found a spot to hide, from it, from them, from the fear, slamming myself into the base of a tree. My breath was fast, faster than it had ever been, and I knew I was missing something. What was it?

"Find him Vala," Mama's voice echoed through the woods again, "Find Caleb."

"I'm TRYING!!" I screamed back at her, between a gulp of air and the weeping that came from my chest and throat. My hands grasped something in the dirt. It was metal. Thin metal. Lifting it from the ground I could see the faint outline of a butterfly, touching the tip of a spoon handle. Mama's spoon.

She called out to me once more, "Find Micah, Vala."

"Vala, wake up. Wake up. You're just dreaming. You're okay." I felt Luca's hands wiping the hair back from my sweat-drenched face. I sat up quickly and could see a small patch of light coming through the motel window.

"You were crying. Are you okay?" I ignored his worried whispers, shoving the curtains out of the way so that I could see the entrance sign, *The Creekbeds Motel*, glowing as brightly as ever. I jumped out of bed and could see that Luca and Linc had slept in the bed adjacent to the one I had just been in. The girls must have gone back to our room.

"Vala, calm down. You should get some more rest," Luca looked alarmed as he tried to pacify me, but I was thinking so clearly. I can't believe it hadn't hit me sooner. The clock blinked five fifteen a.m. and I knew the timing was too perfect.

"I have to go, I'll explain everything later." I tried to leave, but he jumped up too.

"No way, I'm going with you."

"What's going on, you two? Are you guys ok?" I had woken up Lincoln, who peeked up groggily from beneath a pile of blankets.

I laughed at how light I felt. "Sorry Linc, I'm Fine! I'll—I'll be back soon! I'll explain everything." I left the room and ran to mine, with Luca trailing behind me. I grabbed the bookbag I'd retrieved from my home so many months before, quickly and quietly, so as not to wake up Sam and Kate.

I threw the bag on the ground outside our room and started rummaging frantically through it, its contents scattering as I went.

"What are you doing, Vala? Seriously, what's going on?" Luca was trying to stay calm, but I could tell that me waking up like this had shaken him. He squatted next to my pile on the ground, trying to grasp some sense of reason from my sudden excitement. I couldn't answer him though. Not until I knew for sure.

My heart beat rapidly and my hair fell wildly into my face as the chaos of the search ensued and my body shook with exhilaration and exhaustion, but I had to find it…

"The spoon. I dreamt about my mom's spoon." I remembered tucking it away in a small pouch, along with… "Here! Here it is. The letter." The letter my parents left for Caleb and I, who knows how long before.

My eyes read through what I already knew in my head and in my spirit, "Find Micah…where the creek bed glows at the mouth! We're here! We've been here all along, Luca. The Creekbeds!"

I pointed at the ridiculous sign in front of our hotel. Our home. I walked by it every day on my way to work at the diner. The sign's mouth glowed with the word *Vacancy* as it had when we first arrived. As soon as he caught on, I scooped the bags contents back inside, grabbed his hand, and ran in the direction of the diner, along the tree line where Luca and I had walked only the day before.

The lights were on and Papa was already setting up for the morning. I could see Sarah through the giant window in a yellow sweatshirt, her hair braided and pulled back to one side as it always was, helping him before school. Bursting through the doors, we likely looked insane. My hair was tangled and drenched with sweat from the nightmare and the run to the diner. Luca's hair was disheveled from sleep, he wore only a pair of basketball shorts and a t-shirt, and I saw now, that in my rush to get the letter he hadn't put on shoes. He was still grasping my hand when I ran to Papa in front of the counter.

Before he could even greet us, breathless and hopeful, I asked, "Papa, what is your name? Your *real* name?"

I inhaled a deep breath, "Are you…Micah?"

And smiling as if he were expecting me all of this time, he answered,

"Yes, Vala, you found me."

Chapter 14

Fully trusting Papa, or Micah, came easily after we learned the truth and pieced together the clues Mama and Daddy had left. Papa couldn't step in for us until he knew for sure we were who he suspected we were. Knowing his real name was the secret password, of sorts, to connecting with other members of the Remnant. He never revealed himself to a possible believer without them first acknowledging his name. He obviously had suspicions about us, which he shared with the Remnant members at the settlement upon our arrival into town. That's when he decided to take us under his wing, to make sure we stayed safe, and to give me a job.

He had known my parents. He had spent time with them, shared meals with them, and acted as a liaison for the members of the settlement they had created. We learned he was not a believer when he knew my parents, just a sympathizer with a love for people. God slowly, but surely, revealed his grace through the many believers he met over the ten years since meeting my parents and the two years of operating with the settlement. It was hard to believe how perfectly orchestrated our arrival in this seemingly small town, just outside the mountain range was. All leading to where we were supposed to be. Leading us to Micah, and leading me one step closer to finding Caleb.

Even though we knew we were going to a much safer place for us, one filled with other believers, leaving our home at the motel was bittersweet. We had become a family within the tight walls of those rooms. We said our goodbyes to Sarah and Papa. It was hard not knowing when we would see them again. Papa insisted we meet John at the diner for our interviews, but arrive early for a breakfast with him. He and Sarah prepared a sendoff meal for us, and prayed for whatever may lie ahead, before we left.

Sarah hugged us all before leaving for school that morning, her eyes brimming with tears as she made her way to me last, holding me tight and whispering before letting go, "I'm so happy for ya'll, Vala. But I'm gonna miss you so much." I felt the same and made sure to tell her. She had become a dear friend, and now I knew, a sister in Christ.

About an hour before the diner opened, John came with two other men that morning to retrieve us, with the intention of asking a few questions before allowing entrance into the settlement. This would provide assurance that we weren't some sort of infiltrators, waiting to give up their location to the Guard. They didn't ask me any questions though. I guess confirmation that I was the Lee's daughter was enough. Sam and Kate were questioned together relatively quickly, with the mention of a couple of Hall family members living at the safe haven. We were so excited at the prospect of the girls being united with family that Lincoln's interview seemed to take no time at all. Luca's though, was strange. It took much longer than the others.

He kept his head down for much of the conversation, something I had rarely seen him do. He was usually so confident and in charge. He looked from my perspective, to be humbled and even a little afraid in his body language. I knew the others were concerned too when their talking slowed down and we all sat silently at one of the booths, waiting for his interview to end. Papa eventually joined John and the other men at the table, but the questioning continued.

"Why is it taking so long?" Kate was getting impatient. We had woken her so early, and I knew she was excited to get to whoever was waiting for them.

"They're just making sure we're all safe to go to our new home, Katie," Sam answered her calmly, and motioned for Kate to lay her head in Sam's lap to rest while they waited.

Linc smiled at them both, and I felt some unspoken exchange happened between he and Sam when he said, "I'm sure everything is fine, but I'm just going to see if I can help at all."

I watched and waited, reading Lincoln's body language now, convincing these men that Luca was trustworthy. Linc seemed calm and calculated. He repositioned himself to stand beside Luca at the table, placing his hand on his shoulder reassuringly. Luca looked look up at him briefly and then directed his attention back to the men ahead of him at the table. After an eternity they all stood up, shook hands, and Linc and Luca made their way back to where we had been waiting.

"Okay, we're good to go now," Lincoln declared casually.

"What was the problem?" I looked to both of them. I couldn't understand why they would put Luca through so many questions compared to the rest of us. And why wasn't he looking at any of us now?

Luca went to respond, "Vala, I need to…"

Linc interrupted him, "He just had to explain why no one really knew him from back home. It's hard to prove he is who he says he is with his unfamiliarity. But, Papa and I vouched for him, so there shouldn't be any more issues."

He nodded at Luca, who then silenced and reached for my hand, "Let's get going before Papa has customers coming in."

Luca pulled me from the booth and though he looked unsure of himself, he confidently directed us all to John and the others, ready to move to our new home.

As everyone gathered our bags and chattered quietly together, I drew Luca towards the kitchen, close to where he had retrieved me when the Guard had come. When we were out of earshot, surrounded by dishes and fresh eggs waiting to be cracked for that morning's breakfast, I asked, "Is everything ok?"

He looked embarrassed and a bit hesitant. "Everything's fine. Like Linc said, they just weren't sure about me."

Searching his eyes for answers, I pressed on, "Wait, you seemed like you wanted to tell me something before."

He took a step closer to me and wrapped a stray hair behind my ear with his fingers, leaving his thumb to rest on my cheek. "Vala, everything is going to be ok. Let's go home, alright?" His quiet reassurance set me at ease again.

We piled into the Grand Prix and began the drive through the winding roads leading into the mountain pass. Luca drove, following John's car, with Linc in the front seat beside him. It was a quiet car ride. Sam and Kate fell asleep propped against one another, and I took in the beauty of the canyon. Leaves were starting to change colors, as October approached, and the rich yellows, oranges, and reds made the mountains' sides look like they were bursting with flames. I rolled down my window, just a crack, and could feel the air turn more and more crisp the deeper we went into the canyon. Who could find us here? In this vast land of mountains, ravines, rivers, and caves. I found myself wishing whatever the settlement may be, that we could stay forever, but I knew it wouldn't be so. Not while Caleb was out there somewhere.

I caught Luca's glances in the rearview mirror a few times and felt my stomach summersault within me. I hoped we could find time alone soon. We hadn't been alone since Tuesday, in the woods, and I knew he wanted to tell me something back at the diner. It was unusual for him to concede to Linc so easily. As the drive went on, I drifted in and out of consciousness. The warmth of the car and the light pushing through the trees mesmerized me into a good, peaceful sleep. One that didn't wake me with a nightmare of Mama's screams, but rather with Linc telling us to open our eyes as we drove through the compound's gate. The girls were awake too, and suddenly the car electrified with the excitement of what would await us in the safety of the settlement's walls.

The roads were mostly gravel and dirt, and were noisy as we drove through. It was quickly apparent that those living within knew we were coming as they had already stepped out from their cabins to greet us. Some waved while others walked in the direction of the car towards a central point of the camp, to what I assumed was their chapel. We parked where the driveway became a semi-circle and a crowd of people had gathered. As the crowd opened up to welcome our car, I caught a glimpse of a woman I recognized beaming from within, Mrs. Mary Hall.

"Mama?" Kate unbuckled frantically, "MAMA!!"

A foreign sound escaped Sam's throat as she gasped and jumped from the barely parked car, with Kate following at her feet. The girls jumped into their Mom's arms, almost knocking her down with the force of their bodies against hers. My heart simultaneously burst for them while also breaking, wishing it was my own mother waiting with open arms to hold me in. There was cheering from the crowd, crying from the girls, and so much joy as Lincoln joined the Hall's in a never-ending embrace. I stood back beside Luca, treasuring the moment for my dearest friend. My sister. And I thought, *this is what Heaven must look like.*

Chapter 15

THE CAMP WAS HOME TO OVER FIFTY PEOPLE, HALF OF WHICH were children of school age. Some of the children had lost parents as I had. And many of the adults were missing sons and daughters who were taken prisoner by the Guard. The camp's center, reached by the main driveway we drove in on, held the chapel, which also acted as the school during the week. The laundry area, a small cabin beside the Chapel, featured multiple washers, dryers, and a system of clothes lines behind the building for air drying larger items, like sheets and blankets. A meeting hall, a large pavilion, and a cabin that had been converted into a small library sat on the other side of the chapel. Worn gravel roads led from the center of the settlement out like starbursts leading to more wooded areas where cabins had been built to accommodate the refugees. And on the far side of the settlement, past the homes, lay a barn equipped with livestock, a greenhouse, and a large pond, guarded on one side completely by throngs of cedar, oak, and pine trees.

It was easy to fall into life at the settlement. We were secure within the depths of the Appalachian Mountains and with a group of believers we could call family. So many of the inhabitants had known my parents or heard of their courage. I was surprised to find that Mama and Daddy had left more than just a courageous legacy, or a letter, or a secret place for Caleb and I to find a safe haven. They had created a home for us as well. My cabin was small, with two rooms originally intended to house my whole family, a kitchen, a small living room, and a bathroom.

There were traces of Daddy's simplicity and Mama's hand and spirit throughout the cabin. It was warm with quilts I recognized, sewn by my grandmother years before. They were strewn across the beds and the small brown couch that sat beside a large front window, overlooking a beautiful stretch of woods. The golden colors of fall filled my front room, with little need to use the kitchen lights at all during the day. The sun set off of the back porch each night, which stretched the length of the cabin and overlooked a ravine. Five small prints of butterflies were framed along the entrance to the home. A reminder from Mama of the renewal that this place could bring.

Sam and Kate lived with their mother, and their aunt who also found refuge there, in a nearby cabin. Their dad hadn't been seen or heard from since the day the Guard came for us at school, and there was little intel on whether he made it to a camp. After all that had passed, the leaders at the settlement were not hopeful that he had survived. This had been a hard blow for the girls, of course, but they took consolation in knowing their mom had made it. Their reunion with her, and with their Aunt Rachel, had been sweet.

Rachel made it to the camp earlier in the summer, fleeing from her home in the Southeast, near the coast. She was much older than Sam's parents. Her wisdom and kindness shined through bright blue eyes, an eternally warm smile, and soft chin-length, gray hair. When we saw her for the first time, she hugged me as a grandmother would hug a long lost granddaughter. Rachel had never married or had children of her own, yet her years teaching elementary school brought her deep joy. She lacked in nothing, it seemed. I grew thankful almost immediately, to have her company among us.

Kate joined the small school right away and began to live a somewhat normal life as an eleven-year-old girl. We saw her often, skipping down the gravel roads during recess singing *Give Me Jesus* as she went. I taught her the lyrics over the summer. Sam went straight to work teaching at the school with Rachel. She flourished there, mothering so many children who had been upheaved from their life to a strange place, without really understanding why.

Linc and Luca, meanwhile, had no relatives within the settlement, which was full of cabins, but no spare beds. There was word that Lincoln's parents had made it to a settlement further west, bringing him peace, but not tempting him enough to leave Sam. We had heard nothing on Luca's family since arriving and no one else had either. So, it made sense for both of them to stay in the room originally intended for Caleb and I, while I took Mama and Daddy's room.

Luca and Linc's room was small, with simple twin beds and a bed stand between. A blue lamp adorned the top. A shared bathroom adjoined our two rooms. And although the living space was small, they seemed generally comfortable in our home. It was a relief to stay together and I was glad to have them in the cabin with me. I couldn't bear the thought of living there alone or from being separated from any of them.

My room, which had been intended for my parents, held a queen bed and a side table. Mama left a framed picture of our family on a camping trip on the bedside table, awaiting their arrival. Another photograph, of Mama and Daddy laughing in our backyard, hung framed on the wall beside the door. I was home.

Our living situation was unconventional. Especially considering the way I felt about Luca more and more each day, but it really was no different from the months we had spent together over the summer. The rhythm we created in the cabin worked well. Luca and Linc left early each morning, after we all drank coffee and shared breakfast together. They helped on the construction of more cabins before winter. While I helped with the livestock the settlement managed which included chickens, roosters, hens. And I helped with the gardening they established inside of a greenhouse.

On some mornings before school, Kate would meet me at the barn to help gather eggs. She chatted vivaciously and was always eager to lend me a hand. She loved to inspect the different colored eggs the chickens produced.

"You see Lucy over there, Vala," she pointed to her favorite hen, "She gave me the prettiest green and blue egg today. It looked like the color of a moldy jelly bean."

I couldn't help but laugh. Her company on these mornings was always interesting, "And a moldy jelly bean is a good thing?"

"Well, no. But if you took a really *really* bright blue and green jelly bean, and then you left it for years and year and *yeaaaaarrrrs*. That's the color of the egg Lucy gave me today." She distributed eggs into cartons as she talked, putting them in rows based on color.

Most of the cartons were filled with rich brown and cream-colored eggs. Some eggs were speckled with bits of color, but the blues were few and far between.

"Mmmhmmm. I see." I listened as she went on and on. I knew Sam would be there soon to pick her up and I'd need to deliver the eggs to half of the campus' cabins' front steps, before heading to the greenhouse later that day. In the meantime, her company provided silly entertainment for my morning.

She chattered to herself seamlessly, without really needing a response from me the entire time, "...And Lucy's boyfriend, Bruno... he's the big old, grumpy rooster with the red feathers... well, I saw him chasing the hens yesterday around the pond!" She looked up from her work, "Its cold in the barn. Aren't you cold, Vala? Mama says it going to be a long winter...Oh, Hi Sammy!!"

Sam had entered during Kate's mostly one-sided conversation and hugged me. "You girls must be freezing!" She rubbed her hands together, bringing them close to her mouth to blow hot air onto them, "Vala, Rachel said she'd like to join you in the greenhouse today, if you can wait until after school."

I was immediately excited at the mention of spending time with Rachel, "Oh, I'd love that. I don't mind waiting at all. Are you coming too?" I put my arm around Kate, ushering her towards Sam.

"I can't today. I told Mom I'd help her can some vegetables. She's hoping to give them out to some of the neighbors near our cabin." She grabbed Kate's hand after hugging me again.

"Ok. Tell Rachel I'll see her this afternoon. You two stay warm! And...," I shouted out after them as they left, "Kate, thanks for the help this mornin'! I'll keep Bruno out of trouble!" I could hear Kate's glee at the mention of Bruno and her immediate retelling of the story to Sam as they walked in the direction of the school together.

It was getting colder every day. Mid-day was still warm though, and I took pleasure in walking in the sun down the gravel paths to deliver eggs. I carried cartons along in large, green fabric bags, hanging off of both shoulders. Most people stayed busy each day in their various jobs at the settlement, and I was thankful to contribute somehow.

John's wife, Amy, greeted me from the front step of her porch as I brought their carton up, "Mornin', sweet girl. You look like you're almost finished with that lot." She wore a deep green sweater that almost matched my egg bags, and that accentuated her long red hair, which she pinned back on one side.

"Yes, ma'am. You're my last stop." I was glad to see her. She had been so welcoming to us since arriving only weeks before. Like so many of the others we had met since arriving, Amy had known Mama and Daddy well.

She took the eggs I held out to her in one hand and put the other on the small of my back, leading me towards the front door. She welcomed me into their home chatting as she went, "Well don't you have just the perfect timin'. John is inside having coffee with Luca and Michael. Why don't you come on in and join us."

Knowing my plans to be in the greenhouse weren't until later in the day, I happily joined them. I hadn't seen Luca that morning, and I was interested to hear what he was doing with John and Michael.

Michael was John and Amy's adult son. He, like John, was a large man. Both looked like they belonged in the mountains, with full, almost identical brown beards. Their huge statures towered over Amy, who was not a tiny woman herself. While John was shaped full and thick though, Michael was strong and muscular. He was married to a girl a few years older than me, Bethany.

If I hadn't known that Lincoln was an only child, I would have sworn he and Bethany were siblings. She had the same deeply, dark skin tone and amber colored eyes as Linc. She also happened to be brilliant, like Lincoln. She and Michael had a young, rambunctious son named Johnathan, who had his Daddy's figure and his Mama's striking eyes.

Michael quickly embraced Luca and Linc, upon our arrival to the settlement. He was not much older than them and shared a love for Christ and for basketball, as they did. He, too, helped with construction on the cabins and built his own home before Johnathan's arrival last year.

The men all looked up from the kitchen table as I stepped through the door, and Luca stood up to greet me, "Hi. I wasn't expecting to see you this morning." He leaned in and quickly kissed my cheek and whispered closely so that only I could hear, "You look beautiful today."

My cheeks filled with heat immediately, which I tried to hide by turning to leave my shoes at the door step. As I turned around, John left his chair as well to wrap me in an oversized hug, "I'm so glad to see you, Vala. We were just talking about you." He sat back down, giving Luca a pat on the back as he settled into his seat and gestured for me to sit on the couch near them.

Michael gave me a relaxed wave across the table, "Hey Vala."

From the kitchen, Amy called out to me, "Vala sweetie, would you like some coffee or tea?"

I thanked her for her hospitality and nodded, "Yes ma'am. Could I please have a cup of tea."

"Cream and sugar?"

"Yes. That'd be great. Thanks." I redirected my attention back to the three men who had begun talking amongst themselves again. "So, you were talking about me?" I asked curiously, nudging my way into their conversation.

"Yes, we were young lady," John responded to me teasingly, "All mornin'."

Luca looked embarrassed, but had no problem answering my curiosity with an amused grin, "They are trying to convince me to move out of the cabin."

Michael jumped in defensively, "We just said that it'd probably be beneficial to create some space between ya. Ya'll not being married and everything." He was smiling. It was clear they had been bantering about this for a while. "I remember what it was like before Bethany and I were married." He gave Luca a coy wink.

"For goodness sake, Michael," Amy had rejoined the group and handed me a warm mug, "Vala's only 17." She sat down on the maroon couch that was positioned across from the kitchen table and invited me to scoot closer to her. Its cloth, although fading and tattered, was warm and inviting. I wiggled into its deep cushions as they continued to talk around me.

"All the more reason for Luca to find a new place." John was further adamant after the reminder of my age, "We've offered him our couch here. Or Michael and Bethany have offered a cot in the baby's room until something else can be arranged."

A small burst of anxiety set into my chest. Luca had been with me since the woods. Every night since they had found me in that hole. "Wait, you're serious? Are you forcing him to leave?" I asked, afraid at what the answer may be.

John pacified me quickly, "Of course not," he looked back and forth to both of us, "we just want to protect you both."

I looked to Luca for help, "I mean, Linc shares a bedroom with him." I tried to bring the mood back to what it had been when I walked in, "We've got 24/7 supervision. And we've been living together since the spring with no problems."

John laughed slightly. I knew, though, that as he paused, he was thinking through what he'd say next. "Listen guys, I know you still don't know me all that well." He leaned down, his elbows resting on his knees, "A few weeks' time doesn't tell you much about a man. And I know the two of you have been through more together than most of us can imagine."

He looked at me alone now, "But Vala, Joel and Evie...your parents... they did know me. They trusted me." He seemed to mourn my parents as he spoke of them, his eyes cast down for a moment at just the mention of their friendship. "We walked through our own trials together and I would be remiss to neglect the opportunity to take care of you, or to at least try to." He paused before he continued and redirected to Luca, "Luca, son, you know I think highly of you. We've spoken about so much over the past few weeks, and I'd like you to really think about what I'm sayin'. For your's and for Vala's sake."

Luca responded quickly, "John, I give you my word, nothing is happening in that cabin." He looked at me solemnly, "But when Linc moves out I will too."

I knew it was reasonable, but it hurt just the same. Not because Luca was...whatever he was to me, but because I would be alone then. Really alone. Why didn't I have a say in any of this? It was, after all, technically my cabin. Amy gave me a reassuring rub on the back and I looked down into my forgotten tea cup. The tan, now warm liquid, sloshed back and forth as I tightened my grasp around the cup.

John broke the silence, "Well, ok then. The offer still stands, though, if ya change your mind any earlier." Luca stood at his words and pushed his chair in behind him as John reached across the table to shake his hand, followed by Michael. Their deal was done.

We nodded and thanked them all. I wasn't sure where to go from there, after the awkward discussion. I honestly felt annoyed that we had this group debate about my own life, but I knew that ultimately it came from a good place. Luca, sensing my discomfort, suggested he could walk me home before heading to help on a cabin that afternoon. Everyone said cordial goodbyes, as if they hadn't just been casually determining my living arrangements. Michael mentioned that Bethany would be sorry to have missed me, and Amy hugged me as I thanked her again for my undrunk cup of tea.

"You didn't have to leave, ya know," I looked up at Luca as we left John and Amy's porch.

He grabbed my hand in his, weaving his fingers between mine and pulling both our hands up to his chest, "I know, but I was ready. And I wanted to make sure you're alright." He looked at me sympathetically, "You were kind of blind-sighted there, I'm sorry. They've been talking to me about this since we got here."

"Oh," so he wasn't surprised at all, "I'm fine." I gave him a small, reassuring smile.

He didn't buy it, "I know you're frustrated. Just tell me what's going on in that head, Doc."

I traced the scar along his hand with my fingers and couldn't help but smile at the mention of the weekend in the gym. "It's kind of irritating that I don't have a voice in my own life or my own house. I know it sounds ungrateful. *I am* grateful. I don't know. I just—I just feel like the three of you just made the decision for me."

The words tumbled out of me quickly, a trait Luca often brought out in me. "Why couldn't you have talked about this with me? After everything. I— I can't be alone, Luca. I can't. And I should have a say. I should have a voice… and"

"Whoa, I know. I know. You're right." He paused on the path and put his free hand along the side of my face, forcing me to look at him, "You're absolutely right. I should've talked to you. I'm sorry."

I bit my lower lip, trying hard to grip my emotions and my fear. Luca brushed a stray hair behind my ear and rubbed it between his fingers as he spoke, "But Vala, I'm not leaving you alone. Okay? Linc and I will be in the cabin until he and Sam get married. We're still with you."

I nodded and we walked on until Luca dropped me at our front door, leaving to work on a cabin on the other side of the settlement. I entered the empty cabin alone, wondering if the pit in my stomach would be there still, when the time came.

Chapter 16

MY TIME IN THE GREENHOUSE WAS USUALLY PRETTY SECLUDED, but restful and warm. Others worked there at different times throughout the week and maintained it well, and I had been able to learn much about the process and methods by which they were able to keep the plants growing. Working in the barn, or at the greenhouse, allowed me to serve all of the other believers living there, but in the background how I preferred.

The greenhouse itself was a beautiful medley of scrap wood and metal roofing that layered atop piece by piece, encouraging rain to fall off and to the sides. The windows were reclaimed, taken from old buildings and houses that had been abandoned or left at junk yards. They covered all four sides, adjoining side by side to create a strip of glass and panes, and panoramic views from within. The building faced east, looking toward the pond, and allowed sunlight to hit for the majority of the day.

I admired the fruits of the work done within the reclaimed

walls and treasured walking through the rows of benches where lettuce, spinach, broccoli, cabbage, and green beans could be seen growing through the soil. On the outer most rims of the house, blueberry bushes, figs, ferns, and roses were flourishing. An intricate irrigation system had been created using PVC pipes hanging above the plants and connected to a central spicket flowing from the pond, providing a misting when activated.

My job for afternoon would be to prune any of the plants that were in need, to give a light misting to all of the greenhouse's vegetation, and to turn on a small space heater which kept the plants warm on cooler nights. Rachel arrived as I began clipping a rose bush.

"Hi girlie! Whew, I couldn't wait to get here today! Those kids at the school were like wild stray dogs all day. Couldn't keep em' off me." She was excitable. Her gray hair tucked behind her ears and wide smile and she was clearly out of breath from the hike down the path. "Now, where do ya want me?"

I didn't feel I was one to give direction, but I suggested she could start pruning on the green beans. I noticed some of the plants were beginning to sag with the weight of beans hanging from thin branches. We worked in quiet for some time, my mind still on the morning's events at John and Amy's cabin. The roses I fixed my attention to were breathtaking. A few of the bushes were full of blossomed, deep-red flowers, with petals too numerous to count. My favorite bush, though, held cream colored blooms. Some were an even more pure white, with the edges wilting to tan as they fell one by one below the others. The aroma from just these few bushes could fill the entire greenhouse. It was intoxicating.

Rachel stirred me from the trance I had been in, clipping away at their thorny stems, "You sure are quiet today." She moved away from the green beans and began working near the ferns, adjacent to me.

"Yeah. Um, I'm just focused I guess." I wasn't sure how else to answer her, and I was starting to feel frustrated with myself for allowing the conversation from earlier to stir up so much anxiety within me.

She laughed and nudged me in the side, "Thinkin' about that boy of yours, aren't ya?" There was a pep in her voice, " Woowee, Vala, I'll tell ya what. That's one handsome boy. Really, he's a man I suppose. He's so tall and tan..."

She trailed off describing Luca's very many attractive qualities, unaffected by her own admiration of him. "But girlie, one thang's for certain. He's only got eyes for you."

I giggled and looked closer into my flowers, answering her with a bit of embarrassment, "He's not really, mine—I mean, I guess he is, but..."

She interrupted me, "Oh honey, please. He's yours. No doubt 'bout it. Now, tell me how ya'll came to be." She put her hand out for me to hold and led me to a stool near the heater, patting it with her free hand for me to sit. "You could use a little break, and from what Sammy has told me, you yourself have been through quite the tale. I'd like to hear it."

I knew I was blushing, but I started from the very beginning and told her everything: the day at school, the house, the mint timer, even my time in the woods behind my house. I recounted our months living in the motel, when Luca pushed me into the woods that day and when we discovered Micah. It all came spilling out of me, pent up for so long I could have burst.

It felt good to talk to someone. Until then, I hadn't spoken to anyone. I never even spoke to Sam about my first days in the woods, never wanting to relive seeing Mama and Daddy, lifeless and gone. I guess I felt like Sam would look at me with pity, but Rachel made me feel like hearing my story would allow her to know me better. Like it was part of who I was now. And if I was honest with myself, it was. The events that had passed since that day in April were deeply ingrained within me. I knew they always would be.

Rachel listened throughout. Never interrupting or offering

input. A few times she rested her fingers against her lips, deep in thought or distressed, I wasn't sure. When I was finally emptied of it all, she grabbed my hand and looked at me for a long time. And then, turning to her left, she stood up and walked towards the roses I had been trimming before. She knelt down beside the large wooden bin they were planted in and ran her fingers in the dark soil beneath the plant.

"Vala, you see these roses? Have you ever seen a more perfect flower?" Her fingers continued to run through the soil.

I nodded, "Yeah, they're amazing."

"Yes ma'am, you bet they are. This rose bush—how do you think it came to be?" She stopped to smell one. She rested its petals against her upper lip, savoring it for a moment.

"...they were planted?" I wasn't sure how she wanted me to answer. *How did they come to be? Like any other flower grows.*

She sighed aloud, "That's right. This great, full, flowerin' bush was once just a simple, ugly bulb. Someone planted that bulb deep in this dark, cold, dirty soil... alone." She grabbed up a handful of soil for me to see before allowing it to fall back into the pot. "And ya know what? It would've never grown into anythin' if it hadn't been put in that hole in this bin."

She moved back to me and grabbed my hand with her dirty, soil covered fingers, "Vala, God is growin' you baby, through the midst of some dark and lonely and grimy places." She placed her other hand on my cheek and I could feel tears, that I had surely not expected, welling in my eyes, "But sweet girl, somethin' beautiful will come of it all. You can be sure of that." She kissed my forehead and tapped her hands on my legs a couple of times before standing and going back to her work, leaving me speechless, still sitting on the stool.

I left the greenhouse that afternoon, long after Rachel had said her goodbyes, meditating on what she had said to me, *Something beautiful will come of it all.* It was so very much like something Mama would say. Rachel's fingers against my cheek brought the bittersweet memory of my last moments with her, when she rubbed her hand along my face in the midst of the chaos in our kitchen to tell me everything would be ok. But would it? I hadn't believed her then, and things hadn't been okay for so long. But somehow Rachel's words brought a security I hadn't experienced in such a long time. I felt confident that God could bring beauty from all of this.

I walked alone, from the greenhouse to the chapel, where a weekly prayer meeting was held. It was beginning to get dark, but I knew the way well. The night air provided a fresh breath after the various perfumes of the greenhouse, and I was thankful for the time to think and to pray on the way. Various prayer meetings and Bible studies were held multiple times during the week to come together for worship.

As I arrived, Bethany greeted me at the door. Her amber eyes shone with warmth whenever she spoke, "Hey Vala! I heard you had quite the summit of meetings this morning." She laughed lightheartedly and nudged me in the elbow.

A weight had been lifted since talking with Rachel so I responded simply with, "….boys," as I entered into the small meeting room.

Bethany followed me in, keeping one eye on Johnathan who played on the porch floor with a small matchbox car. One of his chubby little arms held his body's balance on the floor as the other moved the car's wheels back and forth as far as he could reach without toppling over.

"You should take it as a compliment, ya know. So many people just want to look out for you. You're well-loved around here." She wrapped her arm around my shoulder and squeezed me lovingly, like a big sister might.

I agreed, smiling as we both watched Johnathan move the car from the floor to his thigh, driving it up and down his legs. Just as Luca came to meet me at the front, she leaned in close and said so that only I could hear, "Next time those boys give you any trouble, you remind Michael of how he used to sneak over to my house in the evenings when my daddy didn't know. That may set him straight."

I couldn't help but laugh as she guided me towards Luca, who had an arm waiting to accept me in. Putting his arm around my waist he asked, "What's so funny?"

I replied, "Oh nothing. Just girl stuff..." as we found our way down the aisle to the seats Linc, Sam, Kate, Mrs. Mary, and Rachel were holding for us.

Prayer meetings usually began with worship songs, which were led by Bethany and one of the younger teenage girls I didn't know well. Scripture was also usually shared which often followed with a short devotional. On many of these nights, the names of believers in camps were read aloud and prayed for. I recognized them from time to time. They were the names of friends I went to school with, adults who had taught Sunday school, my parents' friends, and my friends' parents. It stung every time *Caleb Lee* was mentioned, but it also gave me hope. Caleb was still alive.

I grew more and more anxious to hear about the camp Caleb was being held at, not knowing how we would manage to get him out. The leaders of the settlement, like John and Michael, assured me that they were working on locations and getting as much information as possible. I was inpatient, yes, but could do little else than wait, pray, and trust in the people that my parents had trusted in.

It turned out that Papa actually owned the land we were living on, which was previously a run-down camp ground years before. He visited as often as he could, bringing Sarah along to worship gatherings and prayer meetings. They usually squeezed into the row with us and I loved to hear Papa's deep, rich voice sing lyrics like, *In Christ alone, my hope is found,* and *How sweet it is to trust in Jesus.* His and Sarah's friendship had become even more cherished to me after knowing all they had gone through on our behalf.

My parents worked with Papa, well before the imminent threat to the Remnant was real and before he was even a believer, to establish this safe haven. I couldn't believe the faith that they had shown. I was still sometimes shocked at the secrets they kept from us. But, Mama and Daddy's bravery inspired and humbled me. I felt proud to be their daughter and that their names were known throughout the campground. I also couldn't help feeling like I may be a bit underwhelming to those that knew them so well. I had escaped and survived, yes, but only because I wasn't brave enough to leave the base of a tree. I knew God's purpose for my survival would be made known, but I wondered and prayed often about what it may be.

Chapter 17

The days grew shorter and the nights came earlier, providing star-filled skies over our cabin. We spent most nights with Sam coming over to our cabin for dinner or to study scripture together. We ended those evenings outside, wrapped in homemade quilts and overlooking the ravine from the back porch of the cabin with Luca and Lincoln at our sides. Lincoln often walked Sam home, leaving Luca and I together for short periods alone.

    He and I had fallen into each other so naturally after that night in the woods. It was simple, being with Luca. Simple and effortless. We talked so easily now, openly for hours. I never grew tired of what he had to say. He sometimes grew quiet, though, and pensive, as I had remembered him in school. Something was stirring inside him, especially those nights on the ridge, and I wondered what was going on inside his head. Was he thinking about his own family? Was he thinking about leaving the cabin? Was he worried we might be found? He usually chalked it up to nothing or would make a joke to lighten the mood, but I knew there was something more. And I prayed he'd tell me when he was ready.

On my eighteenth birthday Luca woke me up before the sun rose. "Vala... Vala...Wake up," he whispered gently beside my face, rubbing his fingertips along my arm.

I sat up groggily, "What's going on?"

"Get dressed in something warm and meet me out front." He kissed my cheek innocently and left me in the dark, chilly room to get ready. The late November air brought a cold front. Thanks to the generosity of the people who surrounded us, we had been given clothes and jackets to help us get through the impending winter. I let me hair fall wavy down my shoulders. I dressed in sweats, an oversized long-sleeve shirt, and tennis shoes and grabbed a heavy coat on the way out. Luca waited for me on the porch with a bookbag over his shoulder and a warm coffee cup in his hand.

Handing me the coffee and taking my free hand in his, he seemed nervous. He leaned in, still whispering, "We're going for a walk, if that's okay with you?" I could see his small smile waiting for a reply. I nodded with excited approval. He led us both down the porch steps and towards the woods, pulling me in close to keep warm.

We walked for a while, quietly content, in an area that I hadn't seen before that day. I wasn't sure that we were even within the parameters of the settlement anymore, but I knew I was safe with Luca.

Finally, coming to a pause at the edge of a large cliff where we could walk no further, he said, "We're here," and dug two quilts out of the bag he carried. He laid one quilt on the ground for us to sit on, and the other he wrapped around us both as we sat on the cliff's ledge. I sat up against Luca's chest with his legs outstretched and his arms around me. I nuzzled in for warmth and felt his lips on my head, on my cheeks, on my neck, and then a whisper in my ear, "I love you, Vala."

I was suddenly conscious of the breath I drew in. My heart raced, but my response was easy, "And I love you." It was the first time I had ever said those words aloud to anyone outside of my family. And the first time anyone had admitted them to me.

As the sun rose that morning, he whispered, "Happy Birthday," and I knew nothing could ever be that perfect again. "I know I don't have much to offer you. Especially today. But, I just want you to know that you're it...," he brushed my hair away from my face, "You're it for me—that is. And I'll choose you every day, as long as you'll have me." He was so strong and confident, and yet he seemed apprehensive. Like he was entirely unaware of what he was to me.

I pulled away from him, looking purposefully into his eyes, "Luca, I choose You too." He smiled and I meant it. "Plus, I really do love those scars of yours." We laughed and he leaned down to kiss me. My forehead, my cheeks again, and then my lips. We prayed there together. The Sun's light provided us with more and more warmth as it rose and we rested in it until mid-morning. On the hike home we talked and made plans for the day.

"Vala, what's Caleb like?" A simple enough question, but he said it so strangely. Maybe he was afraid it would upset me to talk about him. He hadn't asked about Caleb since our first walk to the diner together.

I hesitated. *How could I describe him...* "He's brave and kind. He's really outgoing and bolder than I could ever be!" I giggled thinking about his over-confidence. "He asked out Emma Dates last year, as a freshman. Knowing she'd never go out with someone four years younger than her."

"And did she go out with him?" He seemed impressed.

"Ha, no. Definitely not. But it didn't stop him from asking her a few more times." I remembered how shamelessly he had pursued her, never giving weight to their age difference or her indifference to him. It made me smile to think back on how silly he had been over her.

"And, what about…" he paused, "What were your parents like?" He was clearly more apprehensive to ask this question than he was to ask about Caleb, offering his hand to me as we walked.

"My dad was strong. He was a lot like you, actually. He always thought before he spoke and he was gentle, but firm. I always felt like people really respected him, ya know?" He nodded and I continued.

"Mama was a life force to be around. She could excite you with whatever she was excited about. And everything was an adventure to her. She was light. And free. And lovely…" I found myself smiling, "One time, she woke us up in the middle of the night during the summer, just so that we could catch lightening bugs in the back yard. She said they had secrets to tell us. We were so excited I don't think we ever went back to sleep."

My mind trailed thinking of her. I didn't want to lose myself in their losses. Not when the day had been so perfect. So, I redirected back to him, "What about your parents? What were— are they like?" He was quiet for a few minutes. His fingers tightened on mine a bit. Had I hurt him to ask?

"I'm sorry, if you don't want to talk about them we don't have to." I felt guilty for causing him pain just so that I could avoid my own.

"No, we can talk about them," he put his arm around my shoulder, "They are…" He searched for words.

"They're passionate about what they believe in. My dad is strong and a natural leader. He can convince anyone to do anything. Everyone always told me that I look just like him." I listened carefully. He had never spoken about them before. "My mom is loyal and proud. And she'd follow my dad to the end, no matter what. She is always on his side." He respected them. That much I could tell. But his tone was off somehow. There was little endearment in the way he described them.

"Do you have any idea where they could be? I mean, do you think they went back north?" I almost didn't ask, afraid I'd push too hard.

"I have some ideas."

We reached the clearing and could see the Halls, Lincoln, Papa and Sarah on our front porch. "Let's go to your party, okay?" He led me again. I knew, more than ever, he was guarding himself, but from who?

Papa and Sarah greeted us on the porch with pies from the diner. It was a perfect little piece of our home there. And as we made our way inside, I noticed a great bouquet of white roses and ferns sitting on top of the kitchen counter. I looked to Rachel who winked at me slyly and my love for her grew all the more. The Halls gifted me with a homemade journal that Sam crafted herself.

Sam leaned in, after I unwrapped the brown leather journal, bound with hand stitching and pencils wrapped within and said, "I think it's about time you started up again, don't you?" It felt surreal to be reminded of my love for drawing after so much time had passed. I hugged her with an overwhelming gratitude.

Lincoln pointed out the Christmas lights he had stranded on the front porch, dangling from the rafters overhead. "I thought you may like to sit on the front porch every once and a while." I hugged him too, heartily.

I thought my heart couldn't be any more full, until Luca approached me with his gift, "I hope you like it." He handed me a midsized box, wrapped in newspapers and tied with a dark blue ribbon that looked reminiscent of one I remembered seeing adorning Sam's hair. I untied it carefully, aware of the silence in the room and the eyes watching as I stumbled with the wrappings. Opening the lid, I heard the breath I inhaled and willed myself not to cry in front of everyone.

I recognized the dark blue and black lines right away. Dad's flannel shirt had been sewn around a small throw pillow, "I can't believe you did this."

Luca looked at me with a small panic in his eyes, "Oh, Vala. I'm...I'm so sorry." He approached me and tried to shield me from the eyes of the others, whispering lowly, "I thought you'd like it." He put his hand around the back of my head, brushing my hair down as I tried to gather words. "I'm sorry, Vala. I should have asked you first."

I looked up at him and could see the great love he had for me, "No. Luca... it's perfect." Relief covered his face, "Thank you."

I reached from my tip toes to kiss him. He held me close to his chest for a while, forgetting that the rest of the party was still standing behind him.

"Ahem," Linc cleared his throat, "are you guys gonna make me call John?"

The tension cleared in the air and the silence broke as the entire cabin filled with laughter. I looked around at my family of people, standing around in our tiny cabin, the beautiful things coming out of the darkness. It was the happiest I had been in months.

Chapter 18

WORD CAME ABOUT CALEB IN EARLY MARCH. THE LONG winter of waiting for information made me restless, so I clung to the intel with as much optimism as possible. Caleb was being held about thirty miles from Papa's diner, outside of the town we lived in over the summer. Finding out that he had been this close, for all of this time, brought more guilt than I could have imagined. I had been playing house, getting a job, taking care of livestock and plants, and wasting so much time. All while I could have been making plans to rescue him somehow. He was so close for so long. And now new fears were arising within me. *How would I get him out?*

Caleb's rescue consumed my thoughts. John and the other leaders debated plans and strategies on how to retrieve him, along with some others who were prisoners in the same camp. We knew all of them could not be rescued, but we could bring home as many as possible. I was eager to find a way and the strategy meetings that I insisted I should take part in were proving to be slow-moving.

We sat around a table inside the cold cabin used as a meeting space. Heaters were used primarily in residential cabins and couldn't be spared for our small group. Cups of coffee scattered across the table, along with pens, paper, and maps of the area near the diner. My eyes jumped from person to person as ideas bounced around. None better than the next. Michael, who joined most of the meetings, suggested we go at night, arguing that darkness would provide some level of stealth needed for the plan.

John usually facilitated our discussions. He listened patiently and offered up ideas when suggestions were made, "The problem is, son, that we don't know where they are being held within the compound. Going at night would potentially add much more danger. Especially in the winter."

"What about during the day? What days does he work outdoors?" Lincoln interjected. He and Luca decided to join in the meeting tonight, although Luca stayed mostly quiet.

Another man, I didn't know well, answered, "You may be on to something there, Linc." He looked down at a sheet of paper with notes scribbled across it, " Caleb is on a work duty team on the west side of the camp from five a.m. to seven p.m., Sunday to Wednesday. There's a fence surrounding the perimeter by about a mile and three guard posts on the sides."

John interjected, "But what of the others? Are they on the same work schedule?"

It all sounded bleak—impossible even. As the man I didn't know rustled through his papers once more, looking for information on any of the other prisoners we felt hopeful to release, I looked to Luca, whose head was down. He seemed deep in thought. Up until that point he offered no input. He'd been silently observant and solemn.

When he did speak, though, I wished he hadn't. "Listen, I

think this should wait until after the wedding," he said, glancing at Linc. He and Sam were getting married that weekend.

I protested instantly, "What? We can't keep putting this aside. Let's just make a plan here, tonight."

Luca looked at me, troubled, and continued, "Caleb has been there a long time. We don't even know what condition he is in, to make the trek home. Or the health of any of the others."

Some of the others were nodding their heads in agreement. Luca, despondent, looked away from me, and addressed John directly, "And I don't want Vala to be a part of it when we do go."

I jumped up from my seat, startling Mrs. Mary and Amy, who sat silently beside me all night. "Are you *kidding* me, Luca? Seriously? You can't keep me here. I'm going." Mrs. Mary grabbed my hand to placate me, but I ripped it from her, "No. I'm tired of staying quiet while all of you choose what happens to me and *my brother!*"

"You're not going, Vala." Luca managed to look me in the eyes again. Regaining his posture and his usual confidence, " I'll get Caleb back. I promise you. But I can't have you there." His voice was firm and decided. Just as it had been those months before when he agreed to move out of the cabin when Linc did.

"No— no. I need to—you have no right to decide, Luca. None of you do." I looked around the room for agreement from anyone, but help didn't come. "Caleb is my brother. I have to do this, please!" My voice rose louder and grew shakier as I begged the one person I thought would be on my side. Luca looked to Linc beside him for backup.

He gave Luca an understanding look and stood from his seat at the table, in front of me, "Vala, he's right. Luca would be too distracted if you were there. And…" He stopped, and looked at Luca again.

"Don't look at him! Look at me!" I yelled, my voice no longer insecure.

"Okay, okay Ya'll. Let's table this for tonight," John interceded, trying to calm me down. I felt patronized. He held up his hands between us, as if they alone would stop me from leaping over the table to assault Luca and Lincoln, "I think we all need to take a step back for a few days, alright? We'll get Caleb and the others, *after* the wedding. We'll discuss who goes then." And the discussion was over.

Luca looked down again, ashamed. I willed him to look at me, but he wouldn't. Disgusted I left, pushing myself from the table and slamming the door behind me as I left the cabin. I ignored the gentle calls from Mrs. Mary behind me and knew others would soon follow. So, I walked to the woods to be alone. I hiked, with what little light lit the evening sky around me, knowing I had a flashlight in the backpack I brought with me. I soon found myself at the ridge Luca brought me to on my birthday.

We visited the ridge only the weekend before, on a particularly warm day. Sam and Lincoln had tagged along with us for a picnic. After lunching on peanut butter sandwiches, hard-boiled eggs, and blueberries, Sam and Linc explored the area while Luca and I stayed at the ridge in *our* spot.

Luca moved the blanket, placing it as close to the edge as possible and dropped the pencils and notebook Sam had given to me, into my lap. "Okay. It's time," he said with a giant smirk on his face, "I'm ready for my portrait."

I giggled, "Wow. A bit presumptuous, aren't we?! Who says I want to draw you?"

He sat down closely, leaning in next to me, "Don't draw me." He looked out at the vast horizon in front of us, "Draw this." He laid down beside me, arms outstretched under his head, and drifted off to sleep in the warmth of the sun above.

Aside from the distant sounds of Linc and Sam walking through the woods, complete contentment and silence surrounded us. A small breeze passed through the trees and across my face. And I quickly found inspiration in the beauty surrounding us. I sketched lightly at first, finding old familiarity with the movements of the pencil between my fingers and against the page. As the movements became more and more fluid, the lines began to take shape and I easily lost myself in the process. Looking into the distance, smudging the lines and shadows in with my fingertips, and studying and rehashing sections I had started with. The image that appeared on the page was a mere interpretation of the absolute beauty that lay before me. I could never truly grasp what the creator himself had crafted.

I thought of that landscape now, walking along the same ledge, but unable to clearly see the loveliness of the soft horizon line dissolving into the mountain scape in the darkness. The warmth and contentment of that day were seemingly replaced with darkness and disgruntlement. I paced, thinking through all of the things I would say, that I would scream at Luca, when I saw him at the cabin that night. *Why was he doing this? How could he do this? After all of this time, he knew my only goal was to get to Caleb. He knew what this meant. And why did he want to wait?* We weren't making any progress. We waited for months. For an entire year, I waited and searched and prayed that Caleb was even still alive. Now that we knew, he wanted to wait even longer. I didn't want to wait another day! He knew what this would do to me.

Luca wasn't the only source of my frustration, though. I couldn't understand how this group of leaders at the settlement, all of whom I had grown to respect and love, thought they had the authority over my life? On me. Luca, Lincoln, Michael, John— They all had acted as though their opinions and authority were higher than mine. Was it just out of protectiveness? Because they knew my parents and felt responsible for me somehow? I did have high regard for them all not only as friends, but as Godly men who sought to live and lead for the Gospel's sake at all costs. But I knew that my respect for them as leaders did not mean that I had to remain silent. And I wouldn't.

I'm not sure how long I stayed at the ridge that night, but the trees had become outlined silhouettes as I began the hike back home. The sounds of owls and critters settling in for the night distracted me from the bitter cold that approached as the sun went down. The sweatshirt and jeans I wore didn't adequately shield me from the bitter cold of the mountain air. I took turns holding the flashlight with one hand while I nestled the other, fisted in my shirt pocket to stay warm. Numbness overcame my cheeks and nose, and a pit formed in my stomach from hunger.

When I finally reached the cabin, its warmth instantly allowed my body to release the tension of walking through the cold air for so long. My nose and fingers tingled, thawing with the change in temperature.

As I shut the front door, Luca opened his, "Vala, where have you been?" He took a step toward me. I could see Linc, sitting on his bed through the open door. Ignoring him, I tried to walk past.

"Vala, we have to talk about this. Please." He stepped in front of me, blocking the route to my room.

"Why don't you talk to Lincoln. You seem more interested in talking to him anyway."

"I'm sorry, Vala. I really am. I shouldn't have done that without talking to you first." His remorse was clear, but my time in the woods planning what I would say to him couldn't be wasted.

"No, you shouldn't have!" I snapped back, "It'd be nice if you had talked to *me* about *my* brother or about the things you think

I should and should not do. But instead you talked to all of them *again*, about *my* life." I was fuming.

"I know. I *know*. I'm messing this up—I…" He pushed the hair falling into his face back with both hands and kept them on his hand as he paced away from me for a minute, gathering what he would say next. His stature seemed to fill the entire living room.

"There are some—some things I'm worried about. I just don't want you anywhere near that camp. I can't have you near that camp. Can't you understand that?" There was a real fear in his voice and in his eyes as he spoke.

I didn't want to admit it, but I did understand. "Yes, I get that you're worried, but…"

Finding common ground, he inched towards me. "And do you trust me when I say that I want to get Caleb back? I told you I would. Do you remember, when we decided to find him back in the woods? I am going to get him out of there, Vala. I will."

My resolve began to weaken, and he knew it. He swung the bedroom door shut with Lincoln inside, and then jumped back in front of me, grabbing both my cold hands in his. "You're freezing."

He rubbed my hands together and then brought them up to his mouth, kissing my closed fists. I tried to avoid his gaze. My resolve began to thaw too, knowing he was trying to keep me safe. I knew he cared. He leaned down, putting his face in front of mine, forcing me to look at him. "I promise you, I am going to bring Caleb home to you."

I closed my eyes. I trusted him, but I didn't want to dismiss my feelings so easily. "I should have a voice in this, Luca. I *do* have a voice. I just—I need to get some rest."

His body towered over mine and it was all I could do not to fall into it. He nodded, though, in agreement, "Okay. Yes, you do. Can we please talk tomorrow?" He asked me, searching my face for any sign of forgiveness. I nodded, tiredly, and he pulled me into his arms.

"I *am* sorry," he said, softly and contritely. I knew he meant it.

"I know. Let's just talk tomorrow." I pulled away and went to my room, closing the door behind me and leaving Luca standing in the living room alone.

I didn't bother showering. Instead I pulled the quilt lying at the end of the bed around my body and fell into the remaining covers with my head resting on the flannel pillow, hoping the day would melt away quickly. I waited for my body to thaw under the weight of blankets surrounding me and drifted off to the muffled voices of Luca and Linc talking late into the night in the other room.

"Valaaaa. Valaaa, where are you?" Dad called out for me in the woods. I was next to the oak tree behind our house again. Kudzu and vines covered half of the forest floor creeping towards me slowly. I could run in the other direction, towards the house, and the kudzu wouldn't find me there, but Daddy's voice came from the woods. From the wilderness. I was close enough, I thought, to reach him.

I jumped up, determined to get to his voice.

"I'm coming! I'm right here." Suddenly I ran, deeper and deeper into the forest. I reached out to grab a hand. Was it his? It was firm and strong. I looked down and saw the flannel shirt I had given to Luca the first week in the woods. Daddy's flannel shirt. The hand was leading me, deeper into the woods. I know this hand. It's familiar. But whose was it? The flannel disappeared, but the hand remained strong. Stronger even. I felt strong holding it and knew if I held on, I could escape the kudzu, even in the midst of it.

The voice called out to me once more, "I have him, Vala. Hold on to me." The hand clasped tighter to my fingers and pulled.

My eyes opened up to the sun pouring into my bedroom. It was the first time I had dreamt of the woods in months. It was also the first time I woke up after one of my nightmares, to peace. I saw, like every morning, the picture of our summer hiking trip on the bedside table and maybe for the first time, didn't feel my heart break to look at it.

I prayed, earnestly, that morning. That we'd find Caleb, safely. That self-control would reign over me when I normally wouldn't have it. For super-natural strength in the midst of whatever else may come. For the wedding the next day and the marriage of two of my closest friends, my family. For Luca. For our future. For healing and understanding after all that I had walked through, or been carried through by Christ. And that I would honor the Lord and be bold with my voice for the Gospel's sake, and not my own.

It was cathartic releasing everything that I carried with me through the woods all of this time. The fear and frustration that I so often felt weighed down by seemed to wash away. When I finished, I hadn't even realized the tears streaming down my face. The first time they really flowed freely since I found Mama.

I washed up. Ready and refreshed. I trusted that we would find Caleb. But first, we'd celebrate with Linc and Sam. Luca was right, even if I didn't agree with how he approached it. I didn't know why he wanted to put off planning, but we shouldn't put Sam and Linc's happiness in jeopardy or on hold. Pulling my wet hair into a ponytail, I stepped into the kitchen. Linc, Luca, and John sat at the small table drinking coffee. Why was John there? The exhausted looks on the other two's faces told me that they did not sleep the night before.

"Good mornin', Vala!" John was the only one to greet me, although Luca stood quickly as soon as I opened the door and Linc shot me a faint smile from the table. A strange tone hung over the room and I felt like I walked into something serious.

"Morning," I said it, I'm sure, happier than they expected, "is everything ok?"

"Oh yeah, yeah. I was just gettin' goin'. Amy will be wonderin' where I am. Thank you boys for the coffee. We'll see ya'll at the wedding tomorrow!" John nodded to us all as he began to leave, and Linc stood too, leading John to the door. Luca looked down, exhausted, but managed to thank John for coming by before he left.

Shutting the door as John left, Linc looked at Luca and I standing in the kitchen awkwardly and said, "I think I'll go and see my bride. I'll see you guys later." He smiled and left the cabin.

Luca walked towards me and pulled me to the living room couch, a bit unsure of himself. "How are you feeling this morning? Did you get some rest?"

I curled my legs up underneath me, snuggling into the couch a bit. "I'm better." I meant it and I wanted to set him at ease. The dream and my time of prayer had provided much more peace and a release from the anger I felt the night before.

"Is that why you guys were all acting so uncomfortable? I know I was mad last night, but I've had to time to think and to pray. I'm ok. Really. I mean, you were just worried, right?" I was trailing. It didn't seem to encourage him. "Ya know, maybe I can just wait at Papa's diner when you go for Caleb. Or I could drive the car. *I have* driven a getaway car before." I tried to lighten the mood, knowing I shocked him with my anger the night before and continued, "I'll be safe Luca, but I can still help somehow. I just… I just want to be a part of it."

"I know you can help. And you should be able to decide for yourself," he looked down again as he spoke, "I just want you to know that I wasn't trying to hurt you. I don't want to hurt you."

His tone worried me. Why was he acting this way? My hands framed his face, so that I could force him to look at me. "I know that. We're ok. I trust you and I'm sorry we argued. Let's just move forward and plan after the wedding."

He put his hands over mine, "I actually really need to talk to you about some things after the wedding, okay?"

"We can talk now." He wasn't himself. Something was wrong. "Is it about Caleb? Is he okay? Did you find something else out from John?"

"No, no, no. Not at all. I just know that Sam needs your help today. It can wait. John just came to talk with me and Linc about last night. Not about Caleb." He gave me a reassuring smile and looked me in the eye, on purpose, for the first time that day. "We'll have time alone after the wedding. Just you and me, okay?" He rubbed my cheek with his thumb and kissed me softly.

"Okay. If you're sure you're okay?"

"I'm good. We're good." His tone was intense, but confident again, " I love you, Vala."

"I love you too." I searched his faced for answers one more time, but found none.

"Now, go help Sam." He pushed me up, pointing me toward the door. His change of subject didn't go unnoticed. "I'm sure she's waiting for you."

"Okay, I'll see you later then," I said, slipping on my converse at the front door, and leaving Luca alone on the couch. I ran to Sam's, anxious to tell her about the night before and the strange conversation that morning.

Chapter 19

Sam was glowing. Her auburn hair fell wavy past her shoulders and the pale blue, long-sleeve shirt and jeans she wore made her look effortlessly beautiful. I found her and Kate sitting at their Mom's kitchen table, tying together small bouquets of baby's breath and peach-colored snap dragons, which bloomed around the campground early this year. The girl's talked and giggled as they worked, hardly noticing me come in the front door of their cabin.

"Hey guys." I almost hated to interrupt them.

"Vala!" Kate jumped up from her chair, greeting me warmly, "It's been *foreveeerrrr* since I've seen you!" She threw herself into a bear hug.

"Kate, I saw you last week!" I welcomed her hug. She was growing more all of the time. Her mama recently cut her hair into a cute auburn bob, which she tucked behind her ears. It made her look so much older.

"I know, but it feels like forever." She released me and went back to her work at the table.

Sam got up from her spot at the table too. After hugging me hard (it seemed she always knew when I needed it), she turned to Kate and asked, "Katie, we need some big girl time. Mind if Vala and I sit on the porch for a minute?!" Kate agreed, although she wasn't happy. Sam grabbed her coat and basically pushed me out of the front door.

"What happened last night!!?" Her mom obviously told her about the eventful meeting.

"Oh, Sam. It was so frustrating!! I just—exploded. Everything's okay now though, I think. We're going to work out the details after tomorrow." Saying these words out loud reassured me inwardly. *Everything would be okay, right?*

"Linc said he and Luca stayed up the entire night talking. He said Luca was pretty upset," Sam disclosed, uneasily.

I knew things were weird, but Sam confirming my suspicions about their late night raised other questions. "Yeah, I didn't give him much grace last night, but did he say what they talked about?"

"No. Not really. Just that they were trying to work out a solution to get to the Guard camp," she responded, sounding nervous. And I felt guilty. I was potentially sending her new husband out into a really dangerous situation, for *my* brother.

She read my mind as I thought it and tried to reassure me, "Vala, don't do this to yourself. I want Linc to go for Caleb. And he does too. You're our family." She followed sincerely with, "If it was Katie missing, I don't know what I would do, but I know you would be right by my side."

"Thanks, Sammy." I didn't know what else to say. We were supposed to be getting ready for her wedding. The biggest day of her life; and yet, we were chasing the same thing we had been for the last year.

She held my hand, as a sister would, and we talked on the front steps for a while about Luca and I. She was convinced that we would be next to walk down the aisle. I couldn't believe how much I wanted that to be true. We talked about the wedding day schedule, flowers, dresses, and dreamed about the party and dancing afterward.

Mrs. Mary came out after a while and hustled us into the house, "Girls, we've got a lot of work to do. You all can chat while you take care of business, okay?"

And we did. We worked all day between hot tea breaks and conversation. Rachel joined us after teaching at the school that afternoon. Kate had been allowed to skip for the day to help with wedding planning. I couldn't believe the next day Sam would be a bride and a wife. That night I fell into bed, exhausted and happy. There was no sight of Luca and Linc in the cabin, but I assumed the groom may have preparations for the big day too. I slept deeply and dreamlessly.

White Christmas lights dangled from what seemed like every tree limb surrounding the chapel in the settlement. All of the believers living at the campground were attending, and Papa and Sarah came as well. It seemed everyone was excited for a reason to celebrate. We could hear the chatter of the group of voices from outside the chapel. A guitar strummed slowly as we walked up to the chapel doors. Kate first and then me.

Kate wore a deep, purple dress that came to her knees. I helped her sew it months before, and it seemed higher than it was when we finished it. Her hair tied in a low pony tail and hung on one side. She had permitted a pink ribbon with a piece of baby's breath to be tied into it. She excitedly tip toed down the aisle, trying her best to remain poised at first, but giving in to temptation and skipping once she got halfway down. I could hear the occupants inside laugh out loud.

My dress, one Sarah managed to get for me from in town, was blush colored. It fell loosely over my outer arms, with a light v-neck and tight waste, leading to a skirt that fell to my feet. My blonde hair hung wavy and naturally over my bare shoulders. Taking one look at Sam before going in, I reached out my hand to hers and squeezed.

I whispered, "Love you," as I readied myself and adjusted the small bouquet in my hand before entering the chapel.

I couldn't help but smile seeing Linc waiting for his bride at the front of the chapel, with Luca by his side. Both wore dress pants and suspenders, with white button- down shirts. Luca kept his eyes on me the whole time, his hair falling just over his eyebrow, making my heart pound faster than it already was. I was grateful when I finally reached the end of the aisle, knowing all eyes would no longer be on me. Including his.

Sam stepped to the opening of the chapel doors, her mom holding her hand, and the entire body of people within the church held their breath. She was beautiful. She wore no veil, but a crown of baby's breath wrapped around her head, her auburn hair curled beneath. Her dress, given by a supporter in town, was perfect for her. The long, sheer sleeves wrapped into a cream colored bodice which crisscrossed and synched at her waist, accentuating her curves. The train fell modestly behind her, and she walked with grace and excitement to her groom.

When they held hands to exchange the marriage vows, Linc's words caught in his throat as he recited the words after John, who officiated.

Sam though, was solid and eager as she made her promises to Lincoln, "I, Samantha Leann, will love and serve you for all of my days. In sickness and in health. In joy and in struggle. By God's grace and for his glory, I bind myself to you."

When John declared them *Mr. and Mrs. Lincoln Kale, Man and Wife,* the chapel erupted with cheers, and the couple shared their first kiss. Their happiness was contagious, and the joy felt for them by all was genuine. While most of our friends and classmates were finishing their high school career with tests, school dances, and graduation, we had been fighting for our lives and for our families. It was right that we should live. That Sam and Lincoln should live, fully and together.

Their first dance, again to the light strumming of a guitar, was intimate and warm. Sam's hand held Linc's which he pulled close to his chest. His other hand rested on her waist holding her as near to him as he could. They couldn't take their eyes off each other. The song ended and they were led up to the front with Luca and I, where the entirety of the party prayed over their marriage before starting the festivities.

Rachel and Amy teamed up with some of the other ladies to create a meal for the party. We feasted on roasted chickens, vegetables home-grown from the greenhouse garden, bread loaves with broiled cheese encrusted on top, salads, sweet tea and homemade lemonade. When it came time for cake, the bride and groom smashed small pieces of their coffee-infused, three-layered cake into each other's faces. The crowd roared with applause and laughter as Sam and Linc too, giggled between themselves.

The night was full of dancing, laughter, and food. The band played late into the night, with no one wanting the festivities to end. I found Kate asleep on a chair in the corner of the room, and brought her to Mrs. Mary to take home.

"Bless her. She tried to make it," she laughed as she took Kate up in her arms. She looked tiny again, being cradled by her mother.

Luca caught my eye from the other side of the room and gestured for me to meet him. He put both hands around my waist as soon as we came together and whispered so that only I could hear, "Hello beautiful."

I knew my cheeks blushed instantly. "Hi," I held out my hand for him, "Everything was perfect, wasn't it?" I asked him, breathlessly. His gaze on me was intense and I felt myself wishing we could be alone.

"It was," he answered still staring at me, "dance with me?" I nodded in agreement and he pulled me onto the dance floor, holding me tight in his arms with my head resting under his chin. I could feel the rise and fall of his chest as he took a deep breath.

"I want that to be you and I in the Chapel," he lifted my chin to look at him as he spoke, "I want to love and serve you. In sickness and in health. In joy and in struggle. For all of my days. I want to bind myself to you." We stood still while others danced around us. I was speechless. "You don't have to say anything, Vala. I just want you to know my intentions. I want you to know all of me."

What could I say? I wanted all of that. All of him. I answered him sincerely, "That's all that I want too."

He smiled and pulled me in to dance again.

Chapter 20

THE BRIDE AND GROOM WERE SENT TO THEIR NEW HOME, ONLY when everyone insisted that they go. Lincoln and Luca had helped build a modest cabin near mine, for them to settle in. We cheered as they left, after goodbyes and congratulations. As we watched them walk down the path to their new home, Luca grabbed my hand and led me towards our own.

"Luca, what are you doing? We really should help clean up." I felt terrible not staying behind and I was honestly nervous to go to the cabin alone with Luca. His intensity that night had awaken my own, and I was afraid of my lack of self-control.

"I already spoke with John and the others. They know we're leaving early."

He led me onto the gravel path. "And don't worry, Vala," he said, reading my mind, "I've already found somewhere else to sleep for the night."

"What? You aren't staying at the cabin?" I had almost forgotten his agreement with John. This would be my first night alone since we all met in the woods.

"No. I'm not staying at the cabin. I think it will be best if I go and stay with John and Amy tonight. They offered up the couch again."

"Okay. But you'll come in for a bit, right?" I didn't want the night to end.

"Yeah. I will. I still need to talk to you about some things." He walked with purpose, silently the rest of the way.

As we walked into the cabin, he paced around for a moment. He seemed to be collecting his thoughts. I took a spot on the couch, settling in for whatever he needed to say. He pulled a chair from the table towards the couch, finally sitting directly in front of me and rested his elbows on his legs for a minute. I waited. Why was he so somber all of a sudden? His sleeves were rolled to his elbows, his shirt slightly unbuttoned. I could see his chest rising and falling rapidly, and his hair swept across his face after the night of dancing. He was intoxicating to look at, but obviously disconcerted about whatever was going on inside his head. He no longer wore the marks of the joy from earlier, on his face. He was serious.

He was nervous.

He finally spoke, quietly, "Vala, we need to talk about the plan to get Caleb."

"Oh. Okay." Is that all it was? I felt more and more ashamed at my behavior from the meeting earlier in the week. It had obviously caused a ton of stress. I hated that my temper had gotten the best of me. I tried to set him at ease, "I know I was mad, but this can wait until tomorrow. It's really late and I..."

He interrupted me, "No, it has to be now. I told you we needed to talk about this after the wedding. It has to be tonight."

"I didn't think you meant *immediately* after the wedding. Why? Why tonight?" I didn't understand.

He took a deep breath and answered, "The plan won't work,

Vala. None of the plans will. All of the Guard camps are guarded, with heavy weapons. Even if we did manage to get Caleb out, there's a huge probability that we'd lose others in the attempt, or that we couldn't get out ourselves."

"What are you talking about!? Is this why you were talking to Linc and John all night? You don't want to get him at all now?!" I stood up without intending too, not angry, but begging him to see reason, "He's my brother, Luca…my little brother. He's all I have left."

Luca looked up at me, there was more…

I tried to persuade him again, "How do you know it won't work? We have to try. Let's try something else maybe. We can't give up." I bent down in front of him and grabbed his hands, pleading again, "Please. Please, Luca."

He sighed, deeply. "I know it won't work because I know who runs that camp—and I've—I've…"

"You've what?" Confusion was taking over, and I was afraid of what else he'd say. "What is it?"

He relented, "Vala, I've been there before."

Pausing to look away from me, I knew he didn't want to say anything more. He looked down towards his chest, avoiding my eyes. My heart was going to pound out of my chest. I stood back up quickly, letting go of his hands instinctively.

"You've been there before?" I stared at him, willing him to look up at me, "And who do you know, Luca? You said you know who runs that camp. Who is it?"

He confessed quickly, like ripping the band aid from the already festering wound, "My father…My Dad is the commander of Caleb's camp." The room was spinning and I planted myself back on the couch.

He continued, "Both of my parents are members of the Guard. They have been for the past twelve years." His voice was full of shame, "They helped found the initial cause."

"No. No, you're one of the Remnant. You said you don't where they are... How can they..." My eyes closed, processing his words slowly.

"No. I said I had some ideas of where they were," he paused, "but, there's more, Vala. I need to tell you all of it."

I looked at him, ready to take in whatever he had to say. He had lied to me about his parents, what else could there be? He hesitated, taking long, deep breaths, convincing himself to confess to me.

"I was a member of the Guard too. I joined when I turned eighteen."

I interrupted, trying to understand, "But you just turned nineteen. You've been friends with Linc for two years. How..."

He answered, and with it came a plunge further into this reality I could have never anticipated, "I turned twenty-one this summer, not nineteen." He looked at me for a response. One that I couldn't give him. I blank stared back, piecing together the web of lies he had told.

"When I joined the Guard, they convinced me to go back to high school, under the veil of my parents relocating for a job. It was a good way to gain information on Remnant activity. The intent was to redo my Junior and Senior years to gather two years-worth of information for them. That's when I met Linc. When I met you, really."

Things started to rapidly play into my head. Memories of parties that Luca came to. Luca hanging out with Linc all of the time. Him always observing and rarely joining in on the conversations. He was brooding and quiet...two years. Two years ago...

"The party at my house. You came to that. And the raids started right after. That was two years ago." I processed this knowledge out loud.

His head fell again, "Yes."

"And you were an informant on activities. On...on members." I was putting it together for him. The things he didn't want to say.

But he answered, "Yes."

"My family. My family was raided for the first time two years ago. They came into my house. They destroyed our belongings. They invaded our home. My home…"

Silence.

"SAY IT! Say out loud that you were the one," I yelled, willing him to respond.

"I'm sorry, Vala… I…" I heard the lump catch in his throat. And I didn't care. I felt like I had been punched in the stomach.

The air went out of me and I didn't know if I could draw breath on my own. I stood up again and Luca did too, "You're *Sorry?*"

He came towards me, "I came to Christ the next week, Vala. I confessed to Lincoln. He had been my friend, and it destroyed me. What I had done." He grabbed at my hands, "He forgave me. My parents thought I was still Guard until about two weeks before the school raid."

He tried to pull me towards him, to look at him in the eye as he spoke, "I convinced Linc that we had to check on you at the house that day. To check on your family. I wanted to make sure you were okay. I cared about you, Vala. Even then… I…"

Tears were streaming from my face and I was afraid I'd lose all sense of self-control. I pulled away from him, aggressively. I wanted to hurt him. I said what I had knew would cut the deepest, "My parents are dead! They are dead because of…you."

It landed how I wanted it to. He took a step back as if he had been hit by a weight in his gut. He deserved it. And I kept going. "You've never asked me about that day. We've never talked about it. The day I left home," I paused before continuing, hoping his shame would sink in, "Did you know my Mama was pregnant, Luca? Did you see her when you came to *check* on me? Because you *cared* about me?" The sarcasm was sickeningly liberating coming from my lips.

I walked toward him, "Because I saw her. I found her in the floor of my childhood home after it happened. Cradling her swollen belly...I ...I watched behind a tree, like a coward, while my Dad was shot down by some guy in a suit and they just left him there." I could barely finish, "I sat beside his body for hours."

Tears were streaming. I wiped them away, but then more realizations flooded in. "You let me tear myself apart for a year and said *nothing*. You let me love..." I hated myself. I hated him.

"The ATM at the car dealer— they weren't watching all of our banks. They were watching yours. And that's why we couldn't go back for your car. They'd be looking for you, right? And the questions at the diner. Does John know who you are? I'm guessing he does," I answered myself. Luca stood frozen in the middle of the room, unable to look at me.

"Obviously, Linc knows. And Sam... she lied to me too. You all must have had a good laugh about how clueless I've been!" I stepped into his vision, accosting him directly, "How many people did you tell the truth to, before you told me?"

"They were trying to protect you, Vala. I asked them to let me tell you when the time was right." He looked shattered, and I was glad for it. He reached his hand out to me, tears welling in his eyes.

"Don't touch me." I backed away from him, into the only corner between the couch and the chair he had been standing in front of.

"Vala, I tried to tell you so many times. I wanted to tell you," he pleaded with me now. Cornered with nowhere to go, he came to me and put my face into his hands, forcing me to look at him. "Vala, I love you. I love you. If I could take it back I would, but I wouldn't take back anything that I've said to you and everything we've been through. It's all real. I choose you, Vala." He kissed me, imploring me to move past what I knew I couldn't.

I hated him and I loved him. More than I had loved anyone. He had become my best friend. But he was wrong. Everything we had been through had been a lie. I pushed him off. Pushing him hard away from me and then beat my fists against his chest as brutally as I could, until he caught me and we were both sitting on the floor. I sat crumbled and weeping for a minute, hyperventilating. I hated myself and my own ignorance.

"I need you to leave, Luca." I couldn't bring myself to look at him.

"Please, Vala. Please forgive me," he reached for me again, more desperately than before, "If we could just talk and y…"

"Leave!" I forced myself to look into his eyes.

His eyes closed, a tear falling down his cheek, and he nodded. He didn't look brave to me though, as Caleb had, walking me home from school almost a year ago. He was a coward.

I looked away from him. He grabbed a bag from his room that had been waiting there all along. Then he walked towards the kitchen, paused to put something on the table, and walked out.

I lost myself on the living room floor. Weeping until I couldn't breathe, couldn't think. It felt like they had died all over again. Luca, in my mind, might as well have pulled the trigger. The grief was all consuming. The crying paused only when I knew I'd be sick. Running to the bathroom as fast as I could, I threw myself over the toilet and wept there for a while after. I laid on the bathroom floor until I was sure the sickness had passed and then showered, letting the hot water numb me, to drown out the rest of the world. I threw on sweatpants and a t-shirt and noticed a piece of paper, folded on the kitchen table, on my way back to the living room.

I abandoned it there. Whatever Luca left could wait. I didn't care. I cried myself to sleep on the couch that night. Completely alone.

Wrapped in Mama's quilt.

"Vala, take my hand!" I reached as hard as I could. No matter what I did. No matter how fast or far I ran, I couldn't reach it.

His voice rang out again, "Trust me, Vala. Take my hand." I recognized the voice, but it wasn't Daddy's or Luca's or even Caleb's. The kudzu was closing in on me, vines creeping faster and faster with every step I took. I couldn't escape it. I panicked.

He called out for me again, "I'm here. Take my hand." I knew that voice. His voice. It was the voice of the strong hand, leading me through the wilderness. When I remembered and knew I had to find him, he was there, right beside me. Grasping his hand, I clung to him for life, praying he'd help me escape the Vines. Praying he'd take me from those woods, forever.

"I have you, Vala. Hold on to me."

When I woke, I knew the voice belonged not to anyone I had met before. It was God himself, calling out to me.

"Lord, give me faith," I cried aloud, praying that I could

muster any kind of strength. "I'm so afraid and angry and alone. I don't know what to do."

What did he want from me? I was completely abandoned. Everyone had been taken from me. My parents, Caleb, and now Luca. Even Sam, who I knew loved me, belonged with her husband now. No answer came, though, in the stillness.

But there was, in spite of the subsequent turmoil, a peace beyond comprehension.

I had survived. Somehow, through it all, I had made it. God had been gracious. Even if I didn't understand why it was me, out of all my family, that was left. Why God had allowed me to love Luca so fully, only to feel the deep betrayal and pain I felt now. I looked toward the cabin door and noticed the butterflies Mama had hung in the entry way. Something beautiful could come from this pain. His purpose, I knew, would be made known. I remembered my dream.

"*Hold on to me, Vala,*" the voice had said, "*Hold on to me.*"

So, I would.

I couldn't begin to understand Luca or why he lied for so long. Maybe I never would. But I began to analyze myself in the quiet that morning. If he had told me earlier, would it have changed anything? I loved him, but he would still have been the same man that he was before. The one who turned in my family. Luca was the reason I was separated from Caleb and ultimately, the reason I was an orphan. Somehow he was also the reason, in part, that I had been adopted into Linc and Sam and Kate's family. Could I reconcile that in my heart? Where did I go from here? I wasn't sure.

I didn't know how long I sat on the couch, contemplating my heartbreak and righteous anger. The Sun's light had filled the living room hours before. It had to be late afternoon now. I hadn't eaten and I started to feel the effects of hunger and utter exhaustion. When I walked to the kitchen I remembered the folded paper Luca left on the table the night before. Softened a bit by prayer and numb to the pain, I grabbed it up.

A letter. I prepared myself to be heartbroken and angry all over again. And then heard in the back of my head, *"I have you Vala. Hold on to me."*

I had to trust in him.

> Vala,
>
> This past year with you has brought more joy than I ever imagined possible for myself. And with it, because of what I know that I have done, deep regret and shame. I'll never be able to fully reconcile myself to you. I know that.
>
> But I can try to help you get back what you've wanted, all along. A life for a life.
>
> I do love you, Vala.
>
> And I will choose you, every day, for all of my days.
>
> Luca

"For the spirit God gave you is not one of fear, but of power and love and self-control." 2 Timothy 1:7

Below his handwriting lay the number one patch he had torn from his backpack so long ago. A noted scribbled beside it said simply,

To remind you of what you've gained.

I gripped the letter and patch in my hands. He knew. He wrote this letter beforehand, knowing how I would react all along. I felt ashamed. And confused. *A life for a life?* What was he talking about?

"Caleb!" I said, out loud to no one.

I threw on my shoes quickly, slammed the front door behind me, and skipped steps down the porch, running as fast as I could to John and Amy's house on the other side of the settlement.

I banged on their door loudly, screaming for them, "John!!! John! Amy! Someone open up, please!!" I didn't care how crazed I looked to the people who had stopped to watch me from neighboring cabins. I heard screen doors open and shut next door with those wondering what was going on. Sweat covered my face, or tears, I didn't know. "JOHNNNNNN!!!"

The door finally opened.

"Vala, sweetie," John knew what I had come for. He came onto the porch and wrapped me in his arms, like a father would his daughter and I collapsed into them.

"Please John, where is he? Tell me Luca's here." I knew the answer and had sobbed the question into his chest.

He responded gently, "Vala, he planned this weeks ago. By the time he told us, he had already made contact with the camp to arrange it." John rubbed my hair away from my face and I heard Amy join us on the porch.

"No, we can go and get him though, right? It's not too late. We'll make another way to get to Caleb." I looked up at him, "You knew for so long and you didn't tell me. He didn't tell me." I heard John shushing me like he would a crying child, but I continued, "This is why you wanted him to leave the cabin isn't it? We can beat him there. Maybe we could…"

He pulled me away from him, "Vala, listen to me. This was the only way and Luca knew that. I'm sorry."

"No! No, I'll go myself," I argued. My head and hands shaking, I stepped away from him and walked down the porch steps, determined to get to the camp first. Somehow.

Amy walked towards me slowly, "He's been gone for hours,

sweetheart. He wanted to do this for you and for Caleb." She placed her hand hesitantly on my shoulder.

Defeated and broken all over again, I pulled away from them and sat down on the porch steps. My head lay in my hands as I sobbed into them. I was going to lose them both.

John and Amy sat on either side of me, arms around my shoulders. Quiet. Amy caressed my hair and put her cheek against my head, pulling me closer to her. I leaned into her, giving in to the exhaustion and the loss. My brother was gone and now Luca was too. I let him go. I told him to go.

I could hear spring birds whistling before the evening sun arrived. The air was warmer today, even more so than the day before. Spring was coming, bringing a reminder of newness with fresh blooms, warmer air, and green beauty all around. But I couldn't know what possible beauty would ever come of this. Of this pain. I might as well have been back in the hole, in the woods.

I was all too aware of my breaths, uneven and short. And of John and Amy's much more steady beside me. Then…a car's wheels drove up the gravel path, and slowed in front of the cabin's steps.

The car stopped as I forced myself to look up.

And Caleb stepped out.

Free.

About the Author

B.R. Goodwin is an author, artist, wife, and mother to three. She has a Bachelor's in Fine Art and a minor in Religion from Georgia Southern University. Originally from Georgia, she is most at home in the mountains with her family. A lifelong love for story- telling and women's ministry has evolved into a passion to help encourage women to use a bold voice for the Gospel of Jesus Christ.

For more stories and updates from B.R.Goodwin
follow on Facebook at Author B.R.Goodwin
and Instagram at authorbrgoodwin.

Or check out her website at:
www.brgoodwin.com

CPSIA information can be obtained
at www.ICGtesting.com
Printed in the USA
FSHW012019040521
81145FS